I0664829

By JENNI MICHAELS

All in a Day's Work (Dreamspinner Anthology)
Risk & Reward
Sons of the Countryside

Published by DREAMSPINNER PRESS
http://www.dreamspinnerpress.com

SONS OF THE COUNTRYSIDE

JENNI MICHAELS

Dreamspinner Press

Published by
DREAMSPINNER PRESS

5032 Capital Circle SW, Suite 2, PMB# 279, Tallahassee, FL 32305-7886 USA
http://www.dreamspinnerpress.com/

Sons of the Countryside
© 2015 Jenni Michaels.

Cover Art
© 2015 Aaron Anderson.
aaronbydesign55@gmail.com
Cover content is for illustrative purposes only and any person depicted on the cover is a model.

ISBN: 978-1-63216-283-0
Digital ISBN: 978-1-63216-284-7
Library of Congress Control Number: 2014948401
First Edition July 2015

Printed in the United States of America
∞
This paper meets the requirements of
ANSI/NISO Z39.48-1992 (Permanence of Paper).

To Heather Anne. If you were a star, I'd wish on you.

ONE

THE TWO men stood just beyond the warmth of the crackling fire, smoking their pipes and peering up at the fading sun as it slid slowly toward the western sky.

"It's too warm for so much of a fire," one of them said, and the other straightened up, knocked his boot against one of the rocks scattered nearby, and nodded.

"Yeah," he replied. "Summer's early, ain't it?" He was smaller than the first, though they were both rather larger than most men Knox had encountered and certainly far larger than Knox himself. This second man had a meaty face that was flushed red from travel and enormous hands. They hung oddly at the ends of his arms but were quick to both his mace and his longbow. He had closely shorn blond hair and corded ropes of muscles that stood out from his thick, short neck. A deep gouge of a scar that began behind his left ear and disappeared under the collar of his shirt, ending Knox knew not where. He imagined he'd find out eventually—even soldiers had to bathe.

The first man tapped his blunt fingers on his chest and took a deep drag on his pipe. His chest was as broad as a barrel and nearly as thick. His long red hair—the same fiery red as the unkempt beard stretched across his jaw—hung in a knotted braid over one shoulder, and it was tied at the end with a length of dirty fabric. Knox flicked his gaze over the man, cataloging his weapons: two knives, a claymore on his back, and a dagger strapped to his wrist.

1

"Wager we'll be missing this warmth soon enough," the first man said, and they both chuckled, taking drags from their pipes.

"Hungry, boy?"

Knox jerked around and found the third of his traveling party; another huge man with muscles stacked one on top of the other, looming over him with a dented metal bowl in hand.

"Sorry?"

The man shoved the bowl at Knox and smiled, not unkindly, but not the expression of one who craved his interaction either. It was little more than a stretching of his mouth. "Go on," he said. "Eat it. There's carrots in there."

Knox accepted the bowl and cradled it in his hands.

"I'm Brae, by the way. Don't know if I said that."

"Yeah." Knox nodded carefully so as not to slosh the soup into his lap. He didn't want to spoil the stew or his pants. "You did, but I'm not sure I remembered."

Brae nodded and stretched his arms over his head. His back creaked and popped alarmingly—the sound of a man who'd known a rough life and led it still. Of course, most men lived rough lives these days, but Knox had spent most of his nights sleeping on a mattress, thin and narrow as it might have been. These were men who lived by the skin of their knuckles and thrust of their blades. Knox could not force himself not to feel sorry for them.

"I'm terrible with names myself," Brae said. "But that one over there"—he nodded his head toward the red-haired man with the long sword—"that's Cathal, and that bloke with the scar what's on his face, that's Pol. And you're Knox, yeah?"

"Yeah," Knox said. He glanced again at Cathal and Pol, then tipped his bowl up and took a tentative sip of his supper. "It's good. Thank you."

Brae smiled again, broader and somewhat warmer this time. He was missing more teeth than he had left. The ones still stuck in his face were yellowed and looked to have a tenuous hold at best. His hair was as dark as midnight and stuck up from his head in untidy clumps. "We take turns for supper," he said. "You hunt?"

"I do."

2

"Then you cook tomorrow. Kill what you catch. Pol don't like rabbits, but beggars and all that. You lot! The boy and I gonna be eatin' your supper soon you don't come get it yourselves!"

Cathal and Pol trudged back obediently and took seats around the fire pit, settling themselves against some of the large stones scattered round the campsite.

"Tides," Pol said. "I'm bleeding starved."

In the ditches that ran alongside their path, gnarled old roots and branches crawled over boulders and stones. In the rainy season the water overflowed the banks and cut off travel into and out of Cahircluain, the capital city of Ailis. Over the years, travelers had cut runarounds and new paths that led away from the Old roads—those that had been abandoned with the fall of the men who'd settled Ailis decades earlier before the first rising of the beasts—but now that the summer sun had dried the worst of the waters, the wide roads were passable again. It was hard to say which was preferable: the Old roads that were wide and easily traveled, but whose ruins were sometimes overrun with bandits, or the new paths that were more prone to dropping off cliffs or wandering without warning away from civilization and off into a river.

It was quiet around their fire. Birds and foxes twittered and tromped around in the new growth that had struggled up through the remains of the Old forest. The tall, thin pine trees were teeming with life. Insects chirped and squawked while woodpeckers hammered away, happy in the early summer warmth.

Knox tried to focus his attention on his supper, though he dearly wished to examine these men more keenly. Information was as much of a currency as money, but until he knew more, it would be good to keep himself firmly in check. It wouldn't do to seem too eager to do anything, unless that thing was to serve the Council.

That these men were soldiers of the Council was itself enough to warrant utmost caution, and though Knox didn't know much about them, he'd do well not to take their training for granted. He'd known each of them less than four hours, but that was hardly a scratch upon the time they would spend together in the coming weeks. Agents of the Council probably didn't speak of themselves

3

freely, but there was much to be learned of a man simply by watching him. Pol, for instance, was pleased with the ugly scar that cut into his otherwise fine face. He angled his face in a way that made it impossible to miss when Brae or Cathal spoke to him. Knox did not speak to him but felt it was fair to assume he'd receive the same treatment. A battle scar then, or the result of an injury sustained in the line of duty. Not something that had happened within Cahircluain's walls, certainly, for the scar was craggy and uneven, and any physician worth his weight in horse dung could suture better than that, even drunk and half-dead. And it wasn't a knife wound—or a sword. No, a wound from a blade would be more precise and aimed with much clearer intent.

Knox didn't like the direction his thoughts were headed. He turned away before Pol could catch him staring, turning his attention to the stew. It was going cold, but it was still filling and hearty, if not particularly flavorful. Knox had had worse. He swiped the edge of the bowl with his finger and stuck it in his mouth.

"Don't know why we couldn't stay in an inn tonight," Cathal was saying, rubbing a big hand over the top of his head and smoothing back his tangled and windblown hair. "We're hardly outside the Magus ráth. We could turn back a ways. The Council don't have to know about it. And if we're going to be sleeping on the ground for I don't even know long, I wouldn't say no to a soft bed tonight."

"You don't think those innkeepers would get word back if four travelers from the Council stopped over for the night?" Brae asked, and that was another thing to remember. While each of these men was a force unto himself, Brae seemed to be charged—unofficially, perhaps, but charged nonetheless—with keeping the other two in line. Knox glanced at Brae, then tipped the last of his stew into his mouth. "Besides, we ain't stopping here, is we? Got two—what do you reckon, Knox?" He gestured toward the western sky. "Two, maybe three hours of light left."

All three men turned to look at Knox, who froze, then forced himself to shrug deliberately. Until he knew more, he would be wise to be deliberate in his speech and his movements. "No idea," he said. "Two or three hours sounds about right."

4

Pol picked his teeth with a fingernail. After examining the bit of supper he extracted, he shoved it back into his mouth and swallowed it. "You can't tell?"

"When the sun is going to set? No more than you can. And I live south of here, so…." He shrugged again and called a smile to his face. "Your guess is as good as mine."

"We didn't bring you here to guess, boy."

Knox bristled at being called a boy, having twenty years beneath his belt, but challenging any of these men would be a legion beyond stupid. There was an end, and it was Knox's job to work toward that, no matter the obstacles.

"Let's be on our way," Brae said eventually, cutting between the two of them and kicking dirt onto the fire. "Come on, lad."

Their horses were tethered to a nearby oak, within reach of a stream. They'd given up on their own dinner and were dozing contentedly. Only Pol's horse was awake and apparently being tormented by flies. She whined and stamped one back foot, then the other, swishing her tail furiously.

"Tides," Pol muttered, walking straight to her and smoothing her silky mane. "There's a girl, come on now." He turned around and glared. "Are we done blathering here? She hates these damn flies, you know she does."

Chuckling, Cathal swung his bag over his horse's back and climbed up after. He tugged the reins and the horse rounded easily, snuffling his displeasure at being woken from his afternoon nap. "I'm already up here, ain't I?"

There were more than half a dozen settlements in the province and numerous smaller and poorer clachans radiating out in a semicircle around the citadel of Cahircluain. Knox's own settlement of Darry was southwest of Cahircluain, bordering on the edge of the uninhabitable flatlands to the south. To the far north were the mountains of Cairn, which were frozen nearly all year long. Though those mountains were their ultimate destination, it was impossible to know when, or truly even if, they would reach them.

They traveled east. It was no surprise that when they had set out on orders from the Council, Brae had led them that way, going

5

toward Greenfall and away from Darry and any ideas Knox might have had, however ill-conceived, of someone coming to his aid. A band of villagers armed with rocks and sticks wouldn't be fit to battle the Council's soldiers, even if they were stupid enough to try to overwhelm them to take Knox back. And even if they were that stupid, Knox was a quiet sort, and though he had lived in Darry since his birth, there were few in it he could claim for friendship. It ultimately made no difference to Knox which way they traveled, and the ride to Greenfall was only a day, same as it was to Darry and Dunmore and nearly every other settlement in Ailis.

They traveled briskly, sticking close to the crumbling roads that remained of the Old World, stopping once more to let Brae find water for his horse. Then they carried on, Brae cursing at the lost time. Since they hadn't set out from the city until midmorning, chances were they'd be camping that night. The weather looked fine, and Knox hoped the warmth would hold once the sun set.

They had crossed the Magus ráth shortly before stopping for supper, leaving the city behind. The terrain unfurling before them was flat and lush. The meadowlands stretched out alongside them. Knox rode abreast of Brae, keeping Egan at a steady trot. Unconcerned about the forces beyond her understanding, Egan tossed her burnt-ginger mane and pranced across the ground, easily keeping pace with the soldiers' larger horses. Knox patted her neck and threaded his fingers into her silky mane.

"Steady on," he murmured. "That's a girl."

"She's a pretty lass," Pol said begrudgingly. "That's just about the finest coat I've ever seen. Aside from Una here, course."

"Of course," Knox replied. "Una is fine indeed."

Pol puffed up his chest proudly and began to prattle on about Una, about how she was the best and the finest and the most important horse in Cahircluain. He'd once turned down an offer of two sidearms and an entire case of wine for her, and wasn't that something? To get an offer like that on an animal? Knox spared him one ear and a sliver of attention, and paid the rest of it to the passing landscape, cataloging any differences between this land and that of Darry. There were very few, though Greenfall was a bit farther north than Darry and much closer to the sea. The wildlife was much the same as well. Knox called a few of them out of their secret places a time or two, when he sensed those who were easily susceptible to him. He was hesitant to risk startling Una or any of the other soldiers' horses, lest his keepers become aware of what he was doing, so he only coaxed the foxes, birds, and packs of wild dogs into his vision and calmed them, then released them and sent them on their way. There was nothing wrong in it, of course, not now, but Knox's magic had been a tangled secret behind his breastbone for so long that it was nearly impossible to use it freely now, no matter the expectations of those around him.

Before long, the sun dipped over their shoulders and made their shadows long. Brae pulled his gelding's reins and brought him around.

"We should pull off the road before it gets much darker."

"Aye," Cathal said. "We're nearer to the stream around this bend a ways." He led his horse on for a few hundred yards, then turned off the path and made for a flat patch of land with a crumbling brick ruin squat in the middle of it. They set their camp against the easternmost wall, which blocked some of the wind that had started up with the setting of the sun. Their camp, such as it was, was easy to make. Having already eaten and on the cusp of summer, there was little need for a fire, but Knox was a slight man with much less bulk than any of his companions, and with only his thin bedroll to keep him warm, he felt a small fire wouldn't go amiss.

Without waiting for instruction or approval, he gathered a small bundle of wood and fished his flint out of his pocket. He bent low, cupped his hands around the match, and lit the fire carefully. Once it was crackling, he held his hands out over it, breathed in the familiar scent of burnt wood and smoke and earth, and missed his home so fiercely his chest ached with it. Darry would be quickening just about now, thrown into a flurry of activity as Ita and Kane's brood came tearing through the settlement to get home before dark and the Galloways and Bradys tried to separate their children—all ten of them red-haired and lanky and covered in freckles and spots—from one another. More than once the Bradys had ended up with one too many at breakfast the next morning, only realizing when there weren't quite enough eggs that Cayden or Brom had wandered into the wrong home and slept on the floor or squashed onto a pallet with the twins.

He'd never realized until then that no matter how you kept yourself apart, home was a place that crept into your bones and built a fire in your heart.

"You best turn in soon, boy, you don't want to fall off that mare o' yours tomorrow," Cathal said, yanking Knox from his thoughts.

"Right," Knox said. "Of course." He turned and moved toward his bedroll without mentioning that Egan never had and never would throw him, even if Knox was passed out drunk or half-dead. It was more likely his own legs would revolt and wander off without him.

"We'll be in Greenfall early on the morrow," Brae said, folding his arms under his head.

"Aye," Cathal said. "With any luck they'll have seen that beast come through."

"With any luck they'll have shot him dead and strung his mangy corpse up in the square," Pol said. Their laughter drifted up to the dark and rolling clouds, where it was swept away into the quickly darkening sky.

Knox dreamt that night of his father. He sank into the dream like a warm bath; it was a heady thing, being able to stand and look his fill, though Knox knew it was a dream because neither of Uilleam's eyes were blackened and his face was free of the guarded countenance that had settled over him from the moment they'd set out from Darry to Cahircluain.

Knox had always looked like his father. They had the same dark brown hair, though, these days Uilleam's was shot through with gray. They had the same deeply set brown eyes, the same jutting jaw and high forehead. Only Knox's small, upturned nose belonged to Shea, Knox's mother, and she had died so long ago that Knox had gained that knowledge only through his father's rememberings.

"I don't know what to do," Knox said.

Uilleam did not answer.

Knox sighed and feasted upon the sight of his father. In his sleep, he turned his back to the fire and curled in on himself, far too young to be weary all the way through his bones.

THEY ENTERED Greenfall through the main gate of the settlement. It was a lovely patch of earth, green and lush. It reminded Knox instantly of Darry: the broken and busted pavement roads, sheds held together with pieces of scrap metal bolted on here and there, the shouts, murmurs, and laughter of a slowly awakening place. A rough fence marked the perimeter of the settlement, separating the workable fields from the dry flatlands to the south and the cliffs of the sea to the east. A few men mended the fence, laughing and joking as they hammered away. Two women were hanging clothes out on a line, throwing amused glances at the fence menders.

It had rained recently, and the air smelled like earth and new growth. The ruts that cut through the main road were still filled with muddy water. Two tiny boys dressed in nothing apart from ragged, too-small trousers were jumping in and out of one of the puddles, squealing in delight. One held a croaking frog in his filthy fist. His chest was streaked with dirt, and he looked ever so pleased with himself.

Homesickness crashed down on Knox like a thunderstorm. Still, he grinned in spite of himself, because his heart was singing and he didn't care to stop it. He swung his leg over Egan and hopped to the ground. Brae followed, landing beside him with a thump and a splatter of mud. Brae's sword banged into his leg, and the reins of his horse jangled. He cut an impressive figure, to be sure. Knox turned his back on him and headed toward the two boys.

"Hello," he called out, approaching the puddle. "That's a fine frog you've got there."

It seemed the world paused for a slow, collective breath. The two boys stared at Knox, who stared right back. The men building the fence straightened up, and the women paused with their laundry halfway to the line. Behind him, Brae's horse shook her lovely

9

mane. Knox could hear the call of the sparrows and the rushing of the nearby stream. He shifted uncomfortably and touched the back of his neck, unpleased at being the center of attention at any moment, much less this one.

Then one of the men started toward Knox with his hammer in his fist, and everything snapped back into motion with a lurch. Knox's heart stuttered and jumped.

His father. Knox must focus on his father.

"What's your business, stranger?" the man called, his long strides eating up the distance between them.

Knox held up a hand in greeting, but when he turned to check on the soldiers behind him, they were all standing with their hands on their weapons, looking exactly as menacing and terrifying as they were meant to.

"Can you stop that?" he hissed desperately, then turned back.

"I'm Knox Cane," he called. "From Darry. We're just passing through."

Brae stepped forward. "We're on business from the Council."

Knox exhaled, fixing Brae with a frustrated glare.

"Reckoned that," the man said. He stopped behind the boy with the frog and laid his hands upon the boy's slight shoulders. "Gannon, go and find your mother."

"But he likes my frog!"

"Go, Gannon. Haley, you as well."

"But—"

"Go on, now. I won't be telling you again."

Gannon dropped his frog, which croaked in relief and fled as quickly as his squashed legs would carry him. Gannon watched him go sadly, then scampered away, towing a grumbling Haley with him.

"Now," the man said, once he had satisfied himself that the boys were out of what he clearly perceived to be harm's way. Knox wasn't entirely sure he disagreed with him. "What's the Council's business in these parts? We paid our taxes, we did. Counted it out meself."

"Aye, course you did," Knox said. "We don't mean to alarm you. We're passing through and—"

"We're looking for a beast," Brae cut in. "Heard tell he might've been seen round this way."

The man's eyes flew open wide. He lifted his hands like he was warding off a wild animal and began shaking his head from side to side, looking from Brae to Knox, to Pol and Cathal. "We've not had any beasts around these parts in years," he said. "No, sir. We certainly have not. We'd have sent word, I swear it. No one round here wants anything to do with those creatures."

His panic was palpable and catching. Other men began to appear in doorways and windows, trickling toward the commotion, faces drawn tight in concern.

"Of course," Knox said eventually, stepping in front of Brae. "We didn't mean to suggest otherwise. Of course you would have done, and we're simply glad your women and children are safe. Now, could we trouble you to replenish our water supply?"

The man nodded desperately, gesturing over toward the town center. "Course you can. The well's right over there, innit?"

Cathal grabbed Knox's arm in a bruising grip and propelled him toward the well, with Pol and Brae following quickly after.

"What the bleeding hell is the matter with you?" Cathal demanded. He jerked Knox so hard his shoulder wrenched, but Knox bit down on the inside of his cheek to keep from crying out.

"What's the matter with me?" he whispered. "What are you lot doing, riding in here like that? Do you think anyone is going to want to tell you anything, you come in here, swinging your sword around like that? You'll terrify them." He yanked his arm out of Cathal's bruising grasp, nearly gasping in relief once it was free. He rubbed it and shot a furious glare at Cathal, who was leaning against the well with his face drawn into a scowl.

"Oh, I don't particularly care what they want to do," Cathal replied.

"Well, that's bloody helpful. How exactly do you expect to get answers from them?"

Pol chuckled darkly and patted his sword. "They give us answers, or else we take 'em. Now make 'em tell us what they know."

"You want me to just start questioning them? I know you're from the city and maybe things are different there, but people like these, they're a quiet lot. They don't take kindly to strangers barging into town and demanding answers to questions. They don't trust us. It'll take time to get them to open up to us."

"I don't care who they trust, or what they take kindly to. We haven't got time to sit around and put their bleeding minds at ease. Is this a bleeding holiday for you? Make them tell you what they know."

"They're not—hell, Cathal, they're not animals."

Cathal laughed dryly. "They really are."

"I can't just force them to answer me!"

"Then what good are you?" Pol roared. "You'd better figure out a way to make them tell you what we want. If you want to see your father again, that is. And I reckon you do."

Knox's heart lurched. He could barely hear the murmuring of the gathering crowd over the heaving of his own lungs. He shut his eyes and tried to steady his breath, but all he could see was his father, not as he dreamt him but as he was: bound, weakened, and held captive in a dungeon the Council had no business employing against their own men. Uilleam had never been a weak man, but he looked brittle in those irons, bent under their weight and bleeding from the wound on his head.

Knox had to clench his fists against the rage that made his blood boil. "You think I should just, what? What is it you want me to do, Pol? Take their minds and force them to bend for me? If I was truly capable of that, do you think I'd be here now, and my father in Cahircluain? Because if so, you're dumber than an animal. You are. You truly, *truly* are. They're just… they're innocent commoners. They don't know anything."

"Or else they do, and they're traitors to the Council. Now make them tell you what they know. Did you really think we were going to do this with any sort of secrecy? You think the Council gives a fig about that?"

It occurred to Knox, perhaps quite belatedly, how very little of a plan they had and how poorly thought out the little they had actually was. "*How*? This is—I can't—I can't do what you want me to do!" Knox exploded. He grabbed his hair in frustration. "I can't and it isn't my father's fault, all right? I just, I can't. My magic doesn't work the way you're asking. *Please,* just...."

"You look weak now," Pol hissed. "We all look weak. Fucking useless. We should leave you here. Send word back to the city. We told the Council you could do this, and you won't make a liar out of me, boy."

"Enough," Brae cut it. His voice was barely controlled fury. "That's enough right now. We all look foolish. Pol, Cathal. Go and find us somewhere to sleep. Then take the horses to the smithy, see if they've room there."

"But—"

Brae turned cold eyes on Pol. "I said that's enough." Then he turned his gaze on Knox and pinned him as effectively as if he'd taken him down with a blade. "And you, boy. I understand what you're saying about this lot, but you will earn your keep, you hear me? You want to spare your father, you help us find that beast. And then you kill him."

TWO

THEY SET up camp at the outskirts of the settlement under the watchful eye of half of Greenfall's men. The men stared at Knox and the soldiers, giving them as wide a berth as possible as though they all had a catching rotting disease. Knox couldn't blame them. Representatives from the Council never meant anything good. Either they were coming to collect taxes people could scarcely afford, or else they were coming to collect people. Tides, the last time the Council had come to Darry, Knox and his father had left at the business end of a pair of swords, one of them in irons. So, no, Knox didn't blame them. Not at all.

It hadn't always been like this. In stories whispered in the back rooms of local pubs and quiet homes, people told tell of the days nearly twenty years ago when the Council had first seized power. It had been to protect the people, they said. The beasts' rule was absolute, and even if the humans weren't under their authority now, was that a future they wished for? For surely no one could wield that sort of power for long without hungering for more. The beasts had claws and fangs, could rend a man limb from limb, could run ten times as fast as any human. Were the people willing to risk their own lives? Were they willing to risk the lives of their children?

But now the Council's rule was as absolute as the beasts had ever been, and the laws—to protect the people, they'd promised, only ever to protect the people—kept the entire country hovering near poverty. The people were tired and they were frustrated. The

Council was feared and hated in equal measure, and Knox was standing so close to them he was being tarred with the same filthy black brush.

For want of something to do, Knox inspected Egan's hooves, cleaning out any tiny pebbles or stones she'd picked up on their journey. Normally she'd let him know if she was in any pain or discomfort, but uneasy as he was, Knox grabbed onto the mundane activity and set about it with as much enthusiasm as he could muster. Behind him, the villagers muttered and hovered; beside him, Pol, Cathan, and Brae sneered and smirked and fed sticks into their fire.

Knox studied his hands. They were rough, dirty, and calloused. His fingers were long and finely boned. His cuticles, ragged and torn. "So now what?" he asked, looking up from his hands and the little pile of dirt he'd scraped out of Egan's hooves. "What do we do now?"

Brae shrugged. "We wait."

"Wait?" Knox asked. "Whatever for? I thought you said we didn't have time for sitting around."

"We won't be sitting long." Pol gave another of his disgusting grins. He stuck a blade of grass in his mouth and chewed on the end of it. Spit gathered at the corners of his mouth. "Wait till the women put their pups to bed and the men head down to the local for a pint. Then we'll go on out and find out what it is we want to know, innit?"

Knox had to shake his head to make sure he'd heard right. This was supposed to be one of the finest teams in the Council's army, and their grand plan for finding the last remaining prince of the beasts was to get a couple of men drunk and hope some useful information fell out of their heads? "Are you serious?" he asked. "That's your plan? Are you quite serious?"

"A bit a drink makes a man bare his soul," Brae said with a shrug.

"This is—" Knox began, but before he could finish his thought, Pol had swung his fist at Knox's face. The blow hit with the force of a hammer, lighting up the inside of Knox's eye socket. He gasped, hands flying to his face as he tried to turn out of Pol's grasp. But Pol grabbed hold of Knox by the front of his shirt and jerked him off balance, so that the tender skin of his throat was pressed right up against the deadly point of the knife Pol had drawn.

"Pol!" Brae shouted, but Cathal was on his feet, grabbing for Brae and holding him back. Knox froze, his heart hammering in his ears, trying to keep his body under control, trying not to move or shake or even breathe.

"All right," Cathal said finally. "Pol, you made your point."

Pol sneered, twisting the blade just a hair so that Knox felt it prick his skin. A drop of blood beaded up and ran, hot and sickening, down his throat. Knox's stomach heaved. "I dunno," Pol said. "I think I'm still making it."

"That's enough, Pol. We need him."

Pol shook his head and bared his filthy teeth at Knox. "I don't reckon we do."

Knox thought of beckoning Egan over and having her kick Pol's face clear off the rest of his head. Tempting as it was, he was terrified to make any move and risk Pol's blade.

"This is Council's orders, you fool. Don't make me take you back to them in pieces."

Pol leaned into Knox's space, sneered into his face with his yellow teeth and rank breath. Then he shoved him away. Knox swayed on his feet, gasping, nothing but pure stubbornness keeping him standing.

Brae broke loose of Cathal's grip. "Take a walk, Pol," Brae said. He shoved him backwards. "Calm down. And don't forget we're on the same side here." He fixed his gaze on Knox. "Ain't we, boy?"

Knox took in a shuddering breath. He touched his throat. When he pulled his fingers away, they were smeared with his own blood. "Yeah," he lied. "Yeah, of course we are."

IT WAS the smell of freshly baked bread that eventually dragged Knox out of the camp he and the others had constructed. The smell of the bread—warm and sweet and homey—drove him to distraction for the better part of an hour as they gathered stones to make a fire pit and hauled water from the well, but little though he wished for

Brae and Cathal and Pol's company, he found himself reluctant to leave them alone for too long.

The small folded leather maps they were passing back and forth made Knox's fingers itch, but it wasn't likely they'd discuss anything of any importance with Knox listening in, and even less likely they'd offer up the maps for him to study.

Knox could wait. He was adept at biding his time. He'd been doing it all his life, after all. And this journey wasn't likely to end any time soon. So Knox could wait. He'd wait and watch and when the time was right, he'd steal those maps and papers and he'd figure out how to get his father back, damn the Council. And damn the wretched beasts, for that matter.

A small, busy market ran along the back fence of the village. In the center was a well-stocked forge, and Knox would have been happy to lay hands on a weapon of his own, but with no money and nothing to barter with, Knox simply shook his head when the smithy caught his eye and beckoned him over. She grumbled when he passed, turning and walking back to the fire.

Someone had constructed a set of wind chimes out of shards of glass and two old forks; their musical tinkling, which would normally have pleased Knox, was like a thousand shards of glass jammed into his aching eye socket. He ground his teeth and made his way farther into the market.

A few farmers were arranging their fruits and vegetables to showcase their finest, another was restacking finely woven straw baskets and rusted old milk bottle crates, and another was squatted down, running down the lane with a chicken barely escaping the grasp of his chubby, outstretched hands.

"Ya wretched creature!" the farmer shouted, clawing at the air directly behind the chicken's backside. "I'll boil you, I will!"

A few small and muddy children were playing in the street in front of the market. They shrieked and hopped to their feet, giving chase as well. The chicken squawked, spread its wings and, feathers flying, barreled directly at Knox.

"A mad chicken," the farmer screamed. "Mind your ankles, sir, it's a mad chicken!"

Grinning, Knox held out a hand and coaxed the chicken to himself—slowly. Instead of obeying, the chicken came to a dead stop in the middle of the street and stared crazily up at Knox, its beak hanging open.

The farmer plowed into the chicken face-first. The children chasing the farmer jumped up and down, clapping their hands, then scattered quickly when the farmer staggered to his knees, mad chicken clutched firmly in his arms.

"You all right?"

The farmer nodded and sneezed out a cloud of dirt. "Quite, sir. Sorry about that, sir. This damnable bird, you see—"

"It's quite all right," Knox interrupted, because the farmer was patting his pockets and fumbling out a handkerchief, and Knox wasn't at all sure the man could manage a handkerchief, an apology, and the chicken all at once. "Honestly, chickens are always getting the better of me."

It wasn't true, not by a long shot. Knox had been communicating with animals since before he could communicate with his own parents, but it was apparently the right thing to say, because the man nodded and mopped his brow with his handkerchief, sagging in relief.

"I keep telling Quinn we ought to eat this one. More trouble than the eggs she lays, this one is. Just yesterday—Lily, no!—just yesterday she nearly put my son's eye out, she did! He was—Lily, no, stop!"

"May I?" Knox asked. He held his arms out and accepted the chicken the farmer thrust into them. Lily calmed almost at once, clucking meekly. Instantly Knox was flooded with a feeling of relief.

"It's the children," he said. "She doesn't like the children."

The farmer raised his eyebrows. "Lily?"

"Yes." Knox nodded. "That's all. They frighten her. Must you bring her to market? I think if she were able to stay home—and stay away from your son, of course—she'd be quite fine."

The man looked at Knox as if he were demented. "Lily would, sir?"

18

Flustered, Knox shifted Lily back to the farmer's arms. He'd forgotten what it was like to have to explain his magic to someone new.

"Yes," he said eventually. "I… you see… I am able to… that is to say I can… sense things. About animals."

The farmer's eyes widened. "Oh. You mean magic."

"Yes."

"Right. Right, of course. Magic, sir. Quite right. Well, I thank you, sir. I'll be sure to keep her clear of the children, I will, and we'll be right as tides, won't we?" He held the chicken to his breast, stepping carefully backward, drifting slowly away. In a moment, he'd be swallowed up by the shoppers, but before that could happen, Knox found himself calling out, "Wait!"

The farmer froze. "Sir?"

"I just…. It seems odd, doesn't it, that I should know your chicken's name and not yours?"

"Devlin, sir." He tipped his hat and took another step back. "The name's Devlin."

"Devlin!" Knox called. "I do wonder if you could help me. I was drawn to the market by the smell of fresh bread, you see, and now I can't seem to track it down."

"Oh." Devlin paused, then waved his free hand over his shoulder. "That's my wife, Quinn. Bakes the sweetest bread in Greenfall, she does."

"Does she?" Knox cast around, looking at the stalls, but he couldn't seem to find one with bread for sale. "Does she not have a stall?"

"Ah," Devlin said. "Reckon she must have slipped back to the house to put Rian down for a nap, the wee thing."

"Of course," Knox said. He forced a smile to hide his disappointment. His stomach rumbled unhappily, and he blushed, pressing a hand to it.

Devlin looked over his shoulder uncertainly, clearly hesitating. Then he nodded and jerked his head away from the market, toward one of the side streets.

"Come on, then, sir," he said, turning on his heel, and Knox followed.

Devlin's home was a cottage on an uneven stretch of land just west of the town center. The cottage was small, but well looked after, and in good repair. The road that had once led up to it had long been cleared, and the grass that had grown in its stead was a thick green ribbon that cut cleanly up to the door, which stood open, letting in the warmth of the early summer evening.

"Quinn," Devlin called. "I've brought company round, come and see."

They made their way inside, where a round woman with a long blonde braid was bouncing a chubby baby in her lap. She smiled up at Devlin, then scrambled to her feet and bowed her head to Knox.

"One of the men from the Council," she said. She shifted the baby to her hip. He made a blubbering noise and blew a spit bubble down his chin. "Forgive me, sir, I was not expecting—"

Knox cut her off quickly. "No, no," he said, shaking his head, taking his hat in hand. "Please forgive me for intruding. It's only, I was looking for some bread." Warmth spread out over Knox's cheeks as he realized how foolish he sounded. What sort of person barged into someone's house because they wanted fresh bread? Most families in a settlement such as Greenfall weren't accustomed to having guests for dinner, and it could be quite a hardship to do so. And with a new baby to care for. Knox rung his hat and felt like an idiot. "That is to say, I was at the market—"

"You are most welcome here, sir," Quinn said, though the warmth of her words was belied by the way she seemed to be barely holding her body still. He face was white, her mouth a thin, furious line. "And I've only just taken some bread from the hearth. Please, will you eat with us?"

"I—" Knox could not figure out what manners dictated of him. Did he stay and intrude upon their house, though Devlin had clearly been uncomfortable inviting him here, or did he risk offending them by rejecting their kindness, reluctant though it clearly was?

"I insist," Quinn said, taking the choice out of his hand. She smiled grimly. "Won't you sit, sir, please?"

She dipped her head, then disappeared into the kitchen, dragging Devlin behind her.

He took a seat in one of the low chairs, folded his hands in his lap, and waited, feeling like a fool. As he waited, he looked around the room. It was achingly familiar to him. Small and square, filled with wooden furniture and handmade quilts. A deep, rectangular fire pit had been built into the floor of the living room, and it crackled happily. By the door stood a wooden bench and a metal shelf filled with boxes. A basket stacked with blankets and quilts was situated under one of the windows.

"Ba ba ba!"

Startled, Knox looked down to find the baby sitting at his feet.

"Ba!"

Knox laughed. "Hello, there, young man," he said, reaching down to wipe the drool from the baby's chin. He had always loved children. He found them much easier to understand than adults. "Rian, isn't it?"

"Ba! Ba ba da ba!"

"Indeed," Knox replied, nodding seriously. Rian pushed himself up to his knees and dug his chubby little fingers into Knox's knees. Something clattered in the kitchen. "Oh, I see, are you coming up here?"

"—suspicious… were you thinking?" Quinn said furiously.

"What was I supposed to do?" Devlin hissed. "Ask him to leave?"

"—to bring him back here? With Rian?"

Guilt clanged around in Knox's belly. He tried to shut out their argument and instead reached down and curled his hands around Rian's pudgy little belly. He cradled his swaddled bottom and deposited him in his lap. Rian laughed happily and offered Knox a tiny globe of light he'd produced from absolutely nothing at all.

"Oh," Knox breathed. "Oh, *tides.*"

He reached out, inching his hand closer to the light. It was breathtakingly beautiful: pink and shimmery, and when Rian placed it in Knox's palm, it was weightless. Knox looked from Rian to the light, knowing he was seeing pure beauty as he'd never seen it before. He also knew, with absolute certainty, that this was not meant for his eyes. Devlin's hesitance and Quinn's barely disguised fury were suddenly clear.

"Shit. Shit, Rian, no, that's a lad, put that away, yeah?"

Rian smacked Knox in the mouth and scooped another half dozen bits of light out of the air.

"Shit! Oh hell, I'm swearing in front of a baby. Rian, put those away, please." Knox poked at one of the bubbles, trying to pop it, but it simply bounced off his finger and floated toward the ceiling. Rian squealed in delight and clapped his hands, producing even more of the tiny globes of light.

"Shh, Rian, I am begging you!" Knox pleaded, but he was laughing as well, because Rian's delight was contagious, and his magic was beautiful. "Before your parents come back in here. Stop it, just—just stop. Come on, lad, just—oh. Oh tides."

Quinn was standing just inside the doorway to the kitchen, shaking hands pressed over her mouth. Her eyes were crowded with shiny tears.

"Oh, Rian. Rian, no."

"I didn't see anything," Knox said quickly, leaping to his feet and thrusting the baby out. "I should go. I'll go."

"What's—oh, blimey," Devlin said, coming to stand in the doorway behind Quinn. He placed his hands on her rounded shoulders, seeming to anchor himself. "Oh, Rian."

"I didn't see anything," Knox said again, nearly shaking the baby now with how desperate he was to hand him over. "Please, please believe me. There was nothing to see. Here, take him. Take him."

"The Council," Quinn said. She took a hesitant step forward, arms coming up between them. Was the stricken look on her face the fear Knox's own father had lived with his entire life? Knox hadn't been much older than Rian when his own magic manifested itself. Rian was so young, so tiny. How could anyone think that there was any other place for him but his mother's arms?

"I don't work for the Council," Knox said, shoving Rian at her. "I don't."

"They'll take him," she whispered. She closed her hands around Rian's middle and lifted him carefully out of Knox's hands. "He's just a baby."

"I saw nothing," Knox hissed. "There was nothing to see." He looked over at Devlin, who was white as winter's first snow, and shook his head. "I am... so sorry to have intruded upon your home. Please. Let me be on my way."

Quinn was pressing teary kisses to the top of Rian's head. Knox wanted to throw himself out the window.

"They take every Magus at the onset of their magic," Devlin said flatly. "They'll take him. They'll turn him into a weapon."

"Not if they don't know about him," Knox said. "And they won't, not from me."

"But—"

"They took me!" Knox shouted, hating himself all over again when Rian exploded into tears at the outburst. "They took me," he repeated quietly. "My father kept me safe for nearly twenty years, then they came and took me, and they took him. Him in handcuffs and me at the end of a sword. I am theirs now, to use as they please, but this boy...." His voice shook; his hands were trembling. Quinn was sobbing into Rian's curls. "No. They will not have this boy."

He nodded sharply and turned to go. "Good day." He was nearly out the door when it occurred to him to stop and turn back. "Just," he said, hand on the doorframe. "Beware of who knows, I beg you. Do not let this fall upon the wrong ears. You—the Council's reach is far, and their pockets deep."

He dipped his head again and made his way back to camp. His magic raced up and down his spine, prickling as it hadn't done since he was a child. He felt undone, close to the edge of something unknown, and when he saw a glimpse of glowing eyes, he nearly broke his ankle trying to swivel around quickly enough to catch a sight of them.

There was nothing there. Not a glimpse of color, not a flash of light, not even the crunch of feet upon fallen sticks. Knox tried to catch his breath and convince himself his eyes were playing tricks on him.

Once he reached camp, he gathered up his bow and quiver. He took down a dozen quail without stopping, then carried the meat back to the fire. The meal he shared with the others that night tasted like the sole of a boot.

It took two days to question everyone in town and purchase the supplies they needed. Then they broke their camp and set out for another settlement. Knox did not see so much as a shadow from Devlin, Quinn, or Rian. Nor did he see any hint of the flashing eyes that had scared him so. If he tried, he could almost believe he'd imagined them.

THREE

THE DAWN came late, struggling through the hazy clouds that had gathered in the night. Still, Knox had trouble dragging himself from his bedroll. His entire body ached from so many days sleeping on the ground with little more than a blanket between him and the hard earth, and his backside was sore from Egan's saddle. It was odd and unexpected, because Knox was certainly not used to finery, was not accustomed to down pillows and feather beds, but still, the road was taking its toll on him. He ached in places he'd forgotten about.

Knox stretched his arms above his head and yawned, wincing when his jaw cracked. He did not wish to rise. He did not wish to travel. He wished to join his father for breakfast and then help him gather water for the garden.

"Up, boy. You'll be all day about it," Pol said. He kicked Knox on the thigh.

Knox scrubbed his hands over his face, rubbing the sleep from his eyes and tugging on his hair, wishing he dared to reach out, grab Pol's boot, and knock him to the ground. "I really wish you'd not speak to me in the morning."

Pol chuckled darkly. He reached into his pocket and pulled out a bit of salted meat, which he jammed into his mouth. "Is that right, boy?" he asked around his mouthful.

"Well," Knox said, pushing himself up to his feet. "No. I wish you'd not speak to me ever, but if I'm aiming for something within reason—"

25

He anticipated the blow and welcomed it, suddenly furious and itching for a fight, never mind Pol was twice his size and had the temper of a nest of hornets. But Brae was between them before Pol could do more than draw his arm back, grabbing Knox and shoving him backwards so that Knox landed on his ass a good four feet from where he'd been standing.

"I'm near tired of your mouth, boy," he said. "Next time I'll let him swing at you. Now pack up your shit or I'll drag you behind the horses today."

The thing to do was to make himself small and to meekly gather his belongings and follow along behind the others. He knew it was, and he knew his father's life depended upon him doing it, so he balled his anger up and shoved it down deep inside and went to fetch Egan. And if he muttered some creative curses along the way, so be it.

It felt wonderful to climb astride Egan and urge her into a fast run. They wouldn't ride so hard for long, not with so much ground left to cover over the coming weeks, but it was clear they all needed to blow off some steam. Their horses ate up the distance, flying over the rolling green hills. Knox kept a close watch on Egan's feet and legs, watching for signs of discomfort, but she was as happy to be running as he was. The wind that rushed past his face, whipping at his hair and numbing his cheeks, stripped him of his foul temper so that when they finally stopped at midday and Brae herded Knox away from the others for a thumping, Knox accepted it with grace.

"They're not men accustomed to being trifled with," Brae told him. "And you can only push one of them so far before he comes back with a blade, son. Mind yourself."

"Yeah," Pol said, bringing Una around so he was sneering down at Knox from some distance. "Mind yourself, *son.*"

It was a stupid thing to do. Knox knew it was a stupid thing to do, and he'd only just agreed with Brae that he needed to keep a better handle on his emotions, but in that moment, Knox found he couldn't stop himself. He let his mind send out a tendril of magic, a tiny little vine of a thing that slipped inside Una's head. Una froze, her ears pricked, and then she sat right down, slowly, so that Knox had a perfect view of Pol's face as he realized what was happening.

"Una!" he shouted, tugging at her reins, but it was no match for Knox's magic. Una huffed, flicked her tail, and planted her butt on the ground. Pol slid off her and landed, ass-first, in an enormous puddle of mud Knox hadn't even seen but was delighted to have found.

"Bloody hell!" he shouted over the sound of Cathal exploding into laughter. "I'll—"

He staggered to his feet, his clothes weighted down with water, muck, and mud, and struggled to unsheathe his sword. Knox didn't have time to be concerned because Cathal was stepping between them, holding out his hands, shaking his head. The grin spread across his face was so broad it must have hurt.

"There now, Pol," Cathal said. "That's good sport, that is. He's only fighting back with what he has."

"Fucking Magus—"

"Aye," Knox burst out. "I am, and you'd do well to remember it. I'm bloody well sick of this. I'm not a child in need of minding. I haven't your sword or your fists, but do you truly wish to push me any further? Because perhaps I can't stop you from running me through with that sword. Perhaps you could put me down where I stand. And I couldn't do anything about it. We all know it. Does it make you feel strong to threaten someone half your size? But I promise you this: without me, you haven't got a chance. You will never find the beast, and you will certainly never capture him. So why don't you do all of us a favor and stop calling me boy. Stop treating me like a child. I'm here. I'm in this. You can stop testing me now."

Knox's chest was heaving by the end of his outburst, and his hands were trembling. It was only Pol's wooden nod that kept Knox from going to his knees under the weight of his own fear.

"Yeah," Pol said. He shoved his sword back into its sheath and turned his back on Knox, who sagged in relief.

After a long, awkward silence, Brae cleared his throat and said, "Unless you lot are eating with the horses tonight, it's someone's turn to hunt."

"Mine," Pol said. His back was a tight, rigid line. He stalked back over to Una, and Knox found the presence of mind to release her from the magic so she returned to her feet, allowing Pol to swap his sidearm for his bow and arrow. No man would waste a bullet on something as mundane as dinner. "There'll be game enough round here."

He tromped over to a nearby thicket of trees; the underbrush was already getting thicker, though they were still far from the northern mountains of Ailis. Knox, still frightened and not a little spiteful, opened his mind, letting it wander.

Pol notched one arrow, and he let it fly toward what Knox could tell was an unsuspecting boar. Knox nudged it and the boar scurried away, leaving Pol's arrow buried in a tangle of thorns. A nearby fox startled, his tiny heart pounding. Knox showed him a hidden stump, and the fox scurried quickly away. Pol exploded in swears. Beside him, Cathal grinned, nudging Knox with an elbow. "Are you doing that?"

"Doing what?" Knox asked innocently as Cathal burst into laughter. Knox followed him over to the flat patch of grass where they were setting up camp, leaving Pol to his hunting.

"That's proper strange," Cathal said. He unrolled his blankets and sat down upon them, reaching for his bag. He pulled out a small leather sack, from which he took his rolling papers and small pouch of tobacco, his thick fingers moving expertly. "Talking to animals like that."

"I guess." Knox shrugged. He sat down as well and stretched his legs out in front of him. It pulled and burned and felt so good after so many hours on horseback. His fury had exhausted him. "I don't really think about it."

"I can see where it might be handy, talking to horses and the like. But I don't think I'd like it. I don't reckon I'd want to know what a doe is thinking before I eat her."

"It's not quite like that," Knox explained. "It's—" He grappled for words, unused to discussing his magic so openly. "It's more subtle than that. Most animals don't have complicated thoughts. Like deer and rabbits and birds. They don't ponder... they're simple creatures, you know? I wouldn't eat a horse, for example. Horses are complicated and loyal. Rabbits just want food and shelter." He shrugged. "So do I. It's just the way of things."

Cathal nodded. "So you wouldn't eat a thinking creature."

"I might eat Pol, push come to shove," he said, and Cathal grinned again, tugging off his boots and setting them out to dry.

Brae grunted and folded himself down onto the ground beside Cathal, worrying at a tooth. "I'm starving."

"Pol's fetching supper."

Brae nodded and leaned back on the grass, crossing his arms under his head. He closed his eyes and sighed up at the sky. "Reckon we can just sleep here tonight. No need to push on."

"Aye," said Cathal. "My bum thanks you."

Brae chuckled. It was the most unguarded Knox had seen him. Even in his sleep, he seemed tense, ready to spring to a fight if it was required of him. But in his rest, he seemed younger somehow, the rough, sunburnt lines of his face smoothing out into something that almost seemed friendly.

"How old are you, Brae?"

"Twenty-six."

Knox raised his eyebrows. "Really? And Pol?"

"Twenty-seven. And Cathal there is twenty-four," Brae supplied.

"Oh." Knox's eyes widened in surprise. Sometimes it was hard to remember that these men were his jailers, that their masters held his father's life in their hands. These men had his father; he must not ever forget that. Not even for a second. "He's only four years older than me."

"Is that right? Well. You look young for your age."

"Well, I'm not built like a bear, if that's what you mean, but I'm not—"

Brae chuckled. "I'm not on about anything. You're just... you're slight, that's all. Reckon you haven't had much reason to train any muscles into those arms of yours."

"I—I—" Knox spluttered indignantly, but he was saved having to answer by Pol tromping back into the camp, a half-dozen dead rabbits swinging from his big fist. He dropped them on the ground at Knox's feet and scowled.

"Well," Brae finally said. "You gonna skin and cook those, or do we eat like beasts tonight?"

"Let the Magus do it," Pol sneered. "He's ever so smart."

"I'm not—" Knox exhaled wearily. "What, do you think I can just make the entire world bend to my whims? I can't just be like, fire, light, wind, blow, and—"

The gust of wind put out the spark of fire almost as soon as it caught, but it didn't matter. It was enough. It was more than. They'd all seen it. Knox slumped down and stared, dumbfounded, into the fire pit.

"Fire," he said carefully. "Light."

The fire jumped to life merrily, shooting up sparks from wood that should have been too wet to light, let alone burn. Cathal gave a low, impressed whistle.

"He speaks to Elements, that one," he murmured, shaking his head. He began dealing the cards out, counting aloud slowly.

"Now," Knox said, and if his voice was trembling, the others were too distracted to notice or too wary to mention it. "Do you want to cook that, or shall I have Una come over here and kick you in the head?"

Pol backed away slowly, throwing Knox an uncertain look as he pulled out his knife and set to the rabbits.

A log shifted in the fire, sending a shower of dancing sparks up into the still night air.

"Like I said," Brae said. "You're not exactly overburdened with the need for muscles, are you?"

Knox lay under his bedroll that night, staring at the stars and thinking of his explosion at Pol. He thought of his father and wished he believed in a god to pray to, that his father would be all right. That this miserable mission would end and quickly, that he might return to the city and see to his father's health. That the beast would be found and that it was as susceptible to Knox's magic as the Council hoped.

And what else could he do with his magic? The wind and the fire, Knox had never experienced anything like it. He had never even heard of a true Magus who could speak to Elements. It only happened in fairy tales and children's stories. Knox closed his eyes and called up a wind, which swept over his face, silky and tempting.

"You doing that?"

Knox turned his head to the side and found Cathal watching him, his eyes bright in the darkness.

"Sorry."

Cathal opened his mouth, hesitated, then closed it again. "That's new, isn't it?"

Knox nodded.

"Blimey. Well. Annoying little shit as you are, I reckon we're lucky you're on our side."

Knox did not reply, just turned his face back to the stars.

"When you meet the beast...." Cathal began. He left the rest unsaid, but Knox heard the question as well as if Cathal had written it out for him. It was the question keeping Knox up nights, staring at the heavens for answers.

"I don't know," he said. "I've never met one."

Cathal rolled over, giving Knox his back. Before long, his soft snores joined Pol's and Brae's, creating a chorus that echoed in Knox's dreams. Knox tugged his blankets up to his chin. It wasn't cold, but he shivered until he fell asleep.

IT WAS quite a thing, traveling with soldiers of the Council. The spring rains had come and gone, and the main roads were beginning to dry out, drawing out traffic and travelers. They came upon them in small groups of farmers with carts of wares they were taking to Cahircluain for market, and families with their children shouting and singing the traveling songs Knox had known since before he could remember. There were even a couple of young men on bicycles, which Knox had heard about but had never actually seen. He dearly wished to get a closer look at them, but he didn't dare ask. When he had traveled in the past, Knox was used to meeting travelers with a

31

smile and a report of the road ahead. These travelers ushered their horses and carts off the road when they saw Knox and the soldiers coming so they could pass unimpeded.

Occasionally Brae or Pol would get it in his head to stop one of the groups and question them. They searched carts and pawed through bags and baskets, and though Knox never dismounted his horse, he felt as though he had black hands each time a woman ushered her children away from their belongings, that they might not be forced to watch them being rifled through.

The travelers all kept their heads down when Knox brought Egan near. He thought he must have stuck out, traveling among the show of strength that was the Council's guard. He dressed the same as the commoners: the stray pair of Old World boots mixed with the boxy, shapeless shifts and pants made from the black wool of their sheep. No one bothered with dying wool for something as simple as traveling clothes. The soldiers, however, wore the bloodred tunics of the Council, and their weapons were fine and ever present. Still the people refused to meet Knox's eyes. Still they kept their heads down, as though he would strike at them for so much as lifting their chins. Knox wondered how much worse it would be if he were dressed in the rich purple of the Magi who lived along the Magus ráth—the magically fortified perimeter of Cahircluain, where the Magi who were taken from their families were raised and trained in the ways of protecting the Council. He hoped he would never find out.

In the days since he'd left Darry, Knox had encountered more people than ever before in his life. Rich men and poor men, farmers and merchants, and women who wore their newborns in slings around their middles. All of them looked upon Pol, Cathal, and Brae with the same look—sick, bitter fear. It was an overwhelming, intoxicating thing. Knox hated every moment of it.

When they stopped to eat—dry brown bread and mealy apples, and oh, how Knox longed for his father's meat pies, for the spiced venison and thick gravy that spilled out the sides and sat heavy in Knox's belly—Pol and Brae wandered off in search of water, and Cathal pulled the leather maps from his bag and bent his head over them. He poked at them, turning them this way and that, looking from one to the other. When he sighed, Knox looked over at him and raised his eyebrows.

"Do you read, Magus?"

Startled, Knox nodded. "Yes."

Cathal passed the maps over wordlessly. Knox took them and bent his head low.

"Those," Cathal said, jamming the map with a dirty fingernail and pointing at a small triangle, "are suspected sightings. And those"—he poked at an X—"are confirmed sightings."

"Of the beast?"

"Of *a* beast," Cathal supplied. He scratched his neck, turning his head this way and that. Knox's own back ached in sympathy. Sleeping on the ground was hard on a body. "We don't know if it's the prince or not."

The top map was a crude thing, drawn with the awkward and careful precision of a child learning his letters. Triangles and Xs littered the landscape, sometimes in clusters, sometimes just a single symbol stuck in the dense western forest or near the cliffs of Ailis. Why people were traveling in those areas, Knox could not imagine.

Beneath that was another map. This one was a finely drawn thing, the leather soft with age and handling, and Knox felt awkward even holding it. He spread it out over his knees and studied it carefully. Cahircluain dominated the center of the map, held safely in the embrace of the Magus ráth. How many people lived and died inside that circle? How many did it willingly? How many knew anything different?

The seven main settlements of Cahircluain sprawled away from the city, spilling to the north, east, and west, toward the cliffs of Akasma and the mountains of Cairn. Darry was small and insignificant, just another black dot amongst the others scattered into the wind. Knox touched it with a fingertip.

"You got a lady back home?"

Knox shook his head. "No."

"You got a lad?"

Heat rushed to Knox's cheeks; he shook his head again. "No."

Knox gazed at the maps for some time. He could not understand why Cathal had given them to him or what he was supposed to be doing with them.

"Where's home for you?" Knox finally asked, refolding the maps and handing them over to Cathal.

Cathal shrugged one big shoulder, casting his eyes over the maps as he stuffed them into the outer pocket of his bag. "Wherever I lay my head, innit?"

"You're not from anywhere?"

"We're all from somewhere," Cathal said, but before Knox could question him further, Pol and Brae came trudging back carrying dripping water skeins. Their clothes clung to them in wet patches, and Brae's black hair stuck to his forehead in wet clumps. Pol's shirt was unlaced, showing that his scar ran down the length of his huge neck, across his sternum, and ended just short of his heart.

"You were all day about it," Cathal told them, giving Brae a friendly shove.

"Found a pond, didn't we?" Pol said. "Colder than a whore's heart, it was."

Cathal rolled his eyes. He slipped his bag over his shoulder and breathed deeply, tipping his head back to the sky. "Rain."

"Aye," Brae said. "We should be on our way."

"You're the one who needed a bath."

"Mind some of us like not to smell like manky old boots," Brae said. He gave Knox a nod and tossed him his water skein. "Not that you'd go in there anyway, Cathal, bog that it was. Couldn't see the bottom at all."

"Hey," Cathal shouted, straightening up. "That's not funny. You never went in a bog, did you? Not this close to dusk."

"We did." Brae grinned and tackled Cathal to the ground, smashing his face into the grass. "There was probably all sorts in there, Cathal. Goblins and the like."

To the side, Pol watched impassively, half-heartedly adjusting Una's saddle as Brae and Cathal wrestled, toppling one another over like school children. They were both grinning, so Knox didn't think it was anything worth breaking up, and he could see why being scared of a bog was cause for a friendly beating.

Until Cathal pinned Brae to the ground and panted out, "The Sidhe, idiot. I don't give a fig about goblins, but you'd do well to mind the Sidhe. A bog, honestly."

"Hang on," Knox said, quickly stepping toward them. "What do you mean, the Sidhe?"

Brae sat back on his haunches, effectively trapping Cathal beneath him. "You've never heard of the Sidhe?"

"Course I have," Knox said. "But they don't live in bogs, do they? Under the hills, innit?"

Brae slapped the ground. "He believes in them too! Pol, are you listening to this? The Magus believes in fairies!"

"They're not fairies!" Cathal said hotly, and Knox jumped in to agree with him.

"The Sidhe are dangerous! You want to get carted off to the Otherworld, do you?"

Brae roared with laughter. "Oh Magus, you are worth your weight in chicken legs, you are. The Otherworld, I ask you."

"You know what it's like with these kids from the settlements," Pol said. "Running around wild with nothing to keep 'em occupied, nothing to stop 'em getting so bored they try and fuck the livestock, innit? Can't have your sons balls deep in the money, so they've gotta keep 'em in line somehow. Scared to death, the lot of 'em. Don't want to get carried off by the fairies and made to live underground the rest of their miserable lives."

"Children's tales, innit?" Brae said, laughing and shoving Cathal to the side. "And you, two grown men still clinging to your mams' skirts about it."

AFTER RECEIVING roughly the same welcome in Dunmore that they did in Greenfall, Knox hung back and let Brae procure an abandoned old cottage for them to sleep in. The small, one-room building was filled with dust and cobwebs; furniture was shoved up against the walls, making the small cottage seem even smaller, but the gathering clouds made Knox glad of the shelter.

Having allowed their horses into the care of two of the local farmers with room enough in their barns and hay enough in their lofts, they were free to set out throughout the village in search of information. Knox detached himself from the group and made his way into a little pub, where he accepted a mug of mead and settled in to wait and listen.

Aside from the unfamiliar faces, Dunmore's pubs were indistinguishable from Darry's. They were loud and crowded, and the lanterns that burned on every table filled the place with a warm light. The wooden floor was covered with mud, straw, and bits of food, and the tables were stained and wobbly.

Knox didn't frequent the pubs that often—drink went to his head and made him woozy, made his magic loose and his lips careless—but it wasn't too difficult to figure out the protocol: drink and gossip. Knox took a seat near a cluster of tables, crossed one leg over the other, grimacing at the crusted mud caking the bottom of his boots, and tried to look like any other traveler seeking shelter and company on a long night. He filled his lungs with the steamy heat of the room and sat back in his chair.

And then a prickle of awareness caught at Knox, causing the tiny hairs on the back of his neck to rise in its wake. He caught his breath, gripping his empty mug with shaking hands, and turned to risk a glance over his shoulder.

A few of the locals were watching Knox and trying to appear that they weren't, but one man was staring at him outright, piercing him with eyes that could have been green or could have been blue, for all Knox could tell. He had dark hair, strong eyebrows, and a full, lush mouth.

Never taking his eyes from Knox's, the man leaned back in his chair and took in a deep breath, his chest rising and falling with the movement.

Knox's skin prickled; his entire body went hot, and he shivered all the way up his back.

"You all right, kid?"

Knox jerked his gaze away from the man and found the barkeep watching him with narrowed eyes. "Aye. Just—someone walked over me grave."

"You want a drink or don't you?"

"Um." One more and Knox was worried he would do something foolish. "Have you got any stew?"

"Course I have. Turnips and carrots and a bit of meat if you're lucky."

Knox's stomach gave a happy rumble. "Could I trouble you for a bowl?"

The man turned and wandered away. Knox wasn't sure if that was a yes or a no.

Without meaning to, he turned again, looking back toward the table where the man sat, but he was no longer looking at Knox. He had turned his attention to his drink and to the man sitting across from him, a thin, dark-skinned man with a shaved head and sharp brown eyes.

" Thursday last," the dark-skinned man was saying. "Should I assume you'll pass that along? Cailean? Did you hear me?"

Cailean nodded. "I'll send word out tonight."

The tiny hairs on the back of Knox's neck stood on end; everyone else in the pub was discussing whose crop was the largest and who had spent the night in someone else's bed, but these men… Knox had the feeling that this was exactly the type of discussion he was supposed to be listening for, but he could hardly concentrate on what they were saying. Something about the man—about Cailean— had caught Knox like a hook behind his sternum and was yanking him from his own mind.

"Here you go, boy."

Knox startled and jerked his head up to find the barkeep shoving into his space with a bowl of stew. He plopped it on the table, dropped a dented spoon beside it, and turned to go. Before he could move more than a step away, Knox reached out and grabbed his arm.

"That—that man," he said with a thick tongue. "Sitting with the dark-skinned man…."

The barkeep narrowed his eyes. "You're with them from the Council, aye?"

"I am," Knox said.

"That dark-skinned fellow is called Jarlath," the barkeep said. "And that one what he's talking to, the Mac Tire, that's Cailean."

"Mac Tire," Knox repeated carefully. He rolled the word around, pressed it with his tongue against the roof of his mouth. *Mac Tire*. It sounded familiar, like a hazy, mostly forgotten memory, but a memory nonetheless. But try as he might, Knox couldn't open up his mouth and ask where the word came from or what it meant. Somehow it was a door he couldn't bring himself to open and walk through. "What are they talking about?"

"Duff," called a voice, and the barkeep made a huffing noise and threw a narrow look over his shoulder.

"What, Fergal?"

"Bring us a round, will you?"

Knox pushed away from his table and turned, glancing over his shoulder to see Jarlath and Cailean making their way across the room. Jarlath was taller, but Cailean was so broad in his shoulders he had to nearly turn sideways to fit through the door.

Duff came back with his hands full of mugs. He splashed them down on Fergal's table.

"Whatcha doin' talking to that Council fellow for?" Fergal demanded, shooting Knox a look that said he didn't particularly care that he was listening or who his traveling companions were.

"He was asking a question," Duff said. He wiped his mouth with the sleeve of his shirt. "They lay down the law, don't they?"

"For near twenty years now. But that doesn't mean you have to—Tides, Duff. You don't have to say everything that comes into your head."

"I was answering the man's question," Duff retorted, but he let the man crowd him away from the tables and into the back of the pub.

Knox should have followed them. Brae would have followed them, same as Cathal and same as Pol. He should have followed them. Instead he finished his soup and slipped out into the rainy night.

He was the first one back to their borrowed house and, having been at the pub for hardly any time, felt safe in sneaking the leather maps out of Cathal's bag. He studied them carefully, trying as hard as he could to locate and memorize the specific outlay of the Magus ráth, where the strongest holds would be, where he might find a weakness. He had no desire to test his magic against those who had been trained in the ways of the Council, but if he had to do it to free his father, he would.

The rain was loud on the roof. Knox lay down on his straw mattress and tried to ignore the flicker that had started up behind his ribs, burning up his insides.

FOUR

"MAGUS!" CATHAL called the next morning, coming over to Knox's bedroll and shaking his wet clothes over Knox's face. "Dry these."

"Ugh," Knox grunted. He rolled over and buried his face in his arms. "Shove off."

"Hey," Cathal said. He shook the clothes again so that they dripped cold, day-old rainwater on Knox's neck. "Hey, Magus."

"Ugh, Cathal, shut up," Knox said, but he flipped over onto his back and reached down inside, calling for a wind.

Cathal arched a bushy red eyebrow. "Any time now."

"I'm trying, Cathal. It isn't working." Knox tried again, but he was too bleary-eyed and sleep-thick to do much of anything except lie on his back and narrow his eyes. "Why isn't it working?"

A scant breeze blew across Knox's face, tickling his nose. "Um."

With a sigh, Cathal dropped his wet clothes in a heap on Knox's face and walked away. Knox groaned, shoved the clothes to the floor, and rolled over to press his face into his arms, but his mattress was wet now, and while Knox could sleep through most anything, he couldn't sleep through that.

"Bloody hell, Cathal." He sat up and reached for his own clothes, grimacing at the way they clung damply to his skin.

"How did it go last night?" Brae asked. "Did you find anyone useful?"

Knox paused, then tugged his pants up over his knees. His palms sweated, but he shook his head and answered, "No, no one."

He found himself in Cathal's company that morning as they knocked on doors and questioned the locals, gathering information and comparing it to things they'd learned the day before and the week before that. Knox was so relieved not to be standing in Pol's shadow that he couldn't bring himself to be upset about not being able to seek out Cailean and Jarlath—the two men from the pub the previous night. It was just as well. What would Knox even say if he did see them? A scarcely overheard conversation and a word that made shivers race down his spine didn't amount to much.

So why, Knox wondered as he followed Cathal from house to house, didn't he ask Cathal about it? If it were anything of note, Cathal would know. If it would help them discover where the prince had fled after escaping the preserve in the northern mountains where the beasts were kept, if it would lead to his capture and Uilleam's life and Knox's freedom, Cathal would know. And it was Knox's duty to the Council to tell him.

The problem was, Knox didn't trust Cathal, and he didn't trust the Council.

For centuries, the beasts had spread across the land of Ailis, ruled by the once noble Phelas. The humans who lived in Ailis governed themselves outside of that rule and paid tribute to the beasts for their protection. None of the surrounding lands dared attack Ailis, guarded as she was by tooth and claw. But some two decades ago, the Phelas grew hungry for power and began dragging the humans under their thumb. A few men gathered in back rooms, and then a few more, and then more still until an army was amassed and the beasts were driven from the cities and into the northern mountains of Cairn, where they lived still. The royal family had been nearly eliminated; only one remained—the last Phela prince.

Those first men formed a Council unto themselves, and from there laws were passed down. From the royal seat of the beasts, they sent out their magicians to create an impenetrable wall of magic surrounding the city. From there, they kept the people of Ailis safe.

At least, that was the story they told in schoolrooms and at dinner tables. Behind barns and under whispering pines, people told a different story, one of a long period of peace and prosperity because the beasts were of magic, and magic loved the land as long as they ruled. Crops flourished and streams ran abundant with fishes. With lips pressed to ears, people told of a power-hungry group of men from the west who had taken the minds of the people, then taken their magicians. Then they'd taken the throne.

Until they'd come to Darry for Knox and his father, Knox had thought these stories he'd heard as a child nothing but silly tales, created because people were cold and hungry and wanted to cast the blame somewhere. But now he found he did not know what to believe or who to trust.

He feared the Council. He feared the beasts even more.

At midday, they met up with Pol and Brae at their borrowed house. Brae had managed to find some paper and was writing a report for the Council in his large, careful handwriting.

The sight of the paper made Knox's fingers itch. The memory of the maps still burned fresh in his mind, and with that thought, he sat down near Brae and offered him his bread. "Shall I help?" he asked, motioning to the papers.

Brae arched a bushy eyebrow. "You write?"

"A bit," Knox said. He took a sip from his stew and tried not to appear too eager. "Thought I might make myself useful."

"Go on, then," Brae said, shoving the papers at Knox. "I can barely read my own hand. Tell them we're on his trail, got the settlers scared out of their wits, eager to help." He took the bread and tore it in half, then shoved a hunk into his mouth. "Make it like we're never out here wasting time. Have any luck today?"

Cathal shook his head, yanking off his sword belt and dropping it to the table with a clatter. "Not a talkative lot, this bunch."

"Same from our side," Brae said. "No one has seen anything or heard anything. Biggest bunch of useless fecks. I'm starting to think Dunmore ought to be laid with a dedicated tax for failing to be useful to the Council."

Pol laughed, a big, hearty chuckle. "Too right. I could use another log on my fire this winter."

"Another fur on my bed, more like," Brae said.

Contempt thundered through Knox. Here these men were, speaking of an unnecessary tax on a poor people, simply for their own amusement. Could they know how these people would struggle come winter? How the men would save their portions for their families and for the women who were with child? Could they possibly know how many children would fail to make it out of the season if they had to offer one more side of beef to the Council? And if they knew, would they even care?

He quickly finished the missive to the Council—beside his own neat hand, Brae's childish letters looked ever more foolish—and folded it. Then he carefully slipped one of the blank sheets of paper out of the stack and folded it as well. He couldn't imagine that Brae had counted the sheets, and if he had, it wouldn't take much to convince him he'd counted incorrectly, not if his arithmetic skills were anything like his writing. He carried them both over to Brae's pack. None of the others were paying him any mind. He quickly separated the papers and slipped the blank sheet into his pocket as he placed the letter with Brae's things.

"Has anyone checked the horses?" Knox asked. No one answered. They were too busy telling bawdy tales of this patrol or that, most of which had to be at least half-false. Knox had a hard time believing Pol could coax one woman into his bed, let alone three at the same time. Knox turned on his heel and made his way across town until he reached the barn where Egan was being kept.

He sent out a thread of greeting before he entered the barn, so by the time he pushed the door open, Egan was prancing in her stall, whinnying happily and stamping her feet.

"Hey, old girl." Knox let himself into her stall and reached for a nearby brush. She'd been combed recently, but she loved the feel of it and it soothed Knox as much as it soothed Egan, so he set about her coat with a shaking hand.

Egan had been with him since she'd taken her first steps on this earth and sensed his discomfort as plainly as a rock under her hoof. She huffed softly and pushed up into Knox's touch.

"I know," he said, leaning against her neck. "I want to get out of here. But we can't, not until we know Father is safe. Now come on, want to come watch me speak to Elements? Apparently that's a thing I can do a bit of."

Egan responded with another whinny and followed Knox out into the pasture behind the barn. The easternmost fence had been left in disrepair and was overgrown by weeds and brambles. Knox made sure Egan knew not to venture in that direction, then forced himself to focus on the rise and fall of his own breathing, the way the wind whispered through the grass, the sweet smell of the fresh soil beneath his feet.

It felt bigger than Knox, the idea of a power such as this—the idea of speaking to the wind or the earth. His magic had always been so small, so specific, but this…. He stopped in the middle of the pasture and motioned Egan away, so she wouldn't get caught up if it went terribly wrong. Of course, given how pathetic his attempts at a wind this morning were, there was probably nothing much to worry about.

"Um," Knox said, lifting his hands out in front of him. "Wind… blow?"

A gentle breeze ruffled the tops of the overgrown grass surrounding Knox, but it was impossible to tell whether Knox had caused it or if it was just a breeze.

"Right. That's… that's fine. A bit more, perhaps? If you please, of course." Nothing happened. Knox sighed and swept his hands through the air, pushing at it as though it were a low hanging branch. "Come on, wind. Let's have a bit of help."

Egan huffed, walked over to Knox, and began nosing at his pockets.

"Egan, go on, girl. Go on over there. I haven't got any sugar. Or are you helping? Is that it?"

Egan huffed again and began nudging Knox back toward the barn. Frustrated at her disobedience and the way his magic didn't seem to be responding the way he wanted it to—which was so unexpected and unusual that Knox didn't know quite how to respond or what to try next—Knox pushed her head gently away and reached for his magic. Egan blew a noisy breath out of her nose and pushed harder, and Knox was so focused on her behavior that he didn't even see it coming. One moment he was trying to stop Egan from knocking him to the ground; the next he was tipped back on his heels with a strong arm crushing his collarbones and a knife at his throat.

"What the—" Knox's arms flew out to the sides, and he windmilled backwards, trying to get away from the knife, but he only succeeded in pushing farther into the grip of the man who was holding him. His boots skittered over the ground, kicking up clouds of dirt and clumps of grass. "What the hell are you doing?"

"Walk back with me nice and easy," the man murmured into Knox's ear, stirring the small hairs on the back of his neck. "That's a lad. Now send your horse away." The knife pressed against Knox's windpipe. "Quietly."

"Egan," Knox choked out. His pulse thundered under his skin, a hair's breadth away from the point of the knife. "Egan, go on, girl, back to the barn with you."

"Use your magic, boy."

Knox forced his hands to unclench, forced his feet to steady beneath him. The man's grip tightened around Knox's throat, and Knox had to swallow down the sob climbing free. His magic began curling into itself the way it did when Knox was preparing to use it; his heart was responding to the orders even when his mind couldn't.

A rush of magic left Knox's body, bursting from his chest and hurtling at Egan. She reared back on two legs and let out a scream, kicking her front legs into the air, then turned and thundered toward the barn. Dirt flew under her hooves.

All of Knox's breath left him at once. He would have sagged in relief, but he was too aware of the blade at his throat to move any more than absolutely necessary.

"What do you want?" he asked, trying to steady his voice. "If it's money, I haven't any."

The man chuckled darkly. "I'm going to take a step back now. And you're going to come with me."

"I'm—" Knox began, but the man stepped back, and the pressure on Knox's throat increased, so he shuffled back as well. "What do you want?"

"I want you to walk back with me," the man replied. His accent was different than any Knox had heard. It was clipped, his consonants harder and sharper than Knox was used to.

"The… the others." Knox's mind raced. Dare he reach out for Una or for the others' horses? Were they near enough for him to reach, and if they were, would he be able to communicate with them enough for them to be of use? There was no way he could communicate with enough intricacy to use them to contact Brae and Cathal. No, there was just Knox and this blade. His magic was of no use. He was helpless. He stared at the barn, but no one came. And the man kept dragging Knox backward. Near the barn, a scream rang out. To the others, Knox begged silently. *Fetch the others.*

"How many are there?"

"Three," Knox gasped. "Three more."

"Their names."

"Brae. Cathal. Pol. I don't know their surnames."

"No, I don't expect you would. Never mind that. They'll be along in a moment, I daresay," the man said, and he was right. No sooner than the words left his mouth, than Brae, Cathal, and Pol were tearing over the fence like the hounds of hell were at their heels.

Pol notched an arrow and let it fly. It soared toward them, directly for Knox's chest, its path so true it might have been drawn to Knox with a magnet. But at the last moment, the man shifted his weight and went to his knees, taking Knox with him. Knox gasped, anticipating the thrust of the blade. Instead he felt the ground as the man rolled them over, keeping their bodies so closely pressed together they might have been one flesh.

Then he reached out and, in a motion that seemed to slow time itself, dug his claws into the ground and hauled them both back to their feet.

"Tides," Knox breathed.

The beast—and it was a beast, Knox realized now; there was no mistaking the claws pricking against his chest—laughed. "Got it now, have you?"

Arrows rained down on them, and the beast dodged them all as if they were slowly falling leaves. Even dragging Knox's body with him, his movements were so quick and so precise, no weapon even came close to them. Eventually the onslaught halted and the beast came to a stop, crouched over Knox's prone body.

Knox could scarcely breathe. He dragged his eyes open and found himself staring up into Cailean's face, hovering inches above his own.

Cailean pressed him harder into the ground, grinding the bones of his wrists together. His cheekbones were smeared with a high flush. Knox's entire body shuddered.

"Stop," Knox gasped out. Then a little louder, "Brae. Stop. Pol, Cathal, please." His chest heaved with each breath, his heart leaping frantically.

Cailean grinned, baring his teeth. "Smart lad," he murmured. He lifted his head, his grip on Knox going tight and unforgiving. "Tell your Council I have the boy."

FIVE

CAILEAN TRAVELED with two other beasts, both women. The first was a tiny whisper of a thing who barely reached Knox's shoulder. Her name was Anne, and she spoke with the same clipped accent as Cailean. Her skin and her eyes were both golden and her head as smooth as a newborn's. She moved with a feline grace, her quick strides belying her tiny size.

The second woman towered over Knox, larger in both height and breadth. She wore very little, her arms and shoulders left completely bare so Knox was able to see the quick play of muscles beneath her pale skin. Her hair hung down nearly to her waist in riotous black curls. She was called Yaara, and the way she showed her teeth when Cailean had dragged Knox back with him made Knox wish his magic *did* work against the beasts. But unless Cailean was highly resistant to it, that didn't seem terribly likely. Knox had tried everything he could think of to force Cailean to release him, and Cailean hadn't so much as flinched. Knox's magic was as useless as a spring breeze against a mighty oak.

He supposed it made sense. Knox's magic had never had the slightest impact on humans, and the beasts were far more human than the stories that preceded them. Almost as soon as they'd left Dunmore, Cailean had shifted, retracting his claws and leaving in their wake very human fingers tipped with very dirty fingernails. And after that, he would have and clearly did pass for any other man. Only the flashing depth of his eyes and the slightly elongated points of his teeth when the light caught them just so spoke of something more.

The crumbling Old World roads that Knox had traveled with Brae and the others seemed to hold no allure for the beasts, nor did the new routes that bypassed the bandit-filled ruins. The beasts traveled on paths apparent only to themselves, stepping without hesitation through brush and brambles that caught and pricked at Knox's pants. Their steps were quick and nimble; Knox felt like a thunderstorm trampling through the brush behind them. Their pace was nearly too quick for Knox to keep pace with, and he found he was grateful for it. If he focused on that, he wouldn't think about his father, or about the Council, or about what they would do now that Knox had been taken by the beasts. He dragged heavy breaths into his lungs and forced his feet to move, his legs to carry him onward. He had no other choice. He would not scream, would not cry, would not falter. His circumstances had changed, but not the plan. He would escape, make his way back to the city, and free his father— somehow.

They wouldn't kill him, surely. They couldn't. It didn't stand thinking about.

"What happens now?"

"If something concerns you, Magus," Anne said, "rest assured we'll let you know."

Anne walked behind him, Yaara to his side. Cailean walked ahead of them, winding his way northeast, moving into the dense forests that would eventually give way to the western cliffs of the Akasman waters. Occasionally Cailean would stop and cock his had to one side, then the other, before altering their course slightly. He spoke very little, and to Knox he spoke nothing at all. But Anne and Yaara followed him without once questioning his path or the occasional instructions he gave.

"Are you the one they seek?"

Cailean didn't miss a step, but his shoulders tightened, and he spoke without looking back at Knox. "I am."

"The last prince of the Phelas."

"Yes."

Yaara glared at him with dark eyes flashing, tugging at her long hair and knotting it at the base of her neck. "We didn't bring you here to ask questions, Magus."

"Then what did you bring me for?"

"Just… keep moving."

They walked for hours. They walked until Knox's hips and feet ached, and his lips were dry and cracked at the corners from thirst. He did not dare ask to stop or ask for a drink. He tried not to think about Egan or what would become of her now; she was a fine horse and would fetch a fair price. Instead he tried to focus on the terrain that passed under his boots as the sun sank ever lower.

It was nearing twilight when Cailean finally brought their group to a stop and began to make camp in a hollowed out bit of land where erosion had taken anything that had once remained of the Old World. Pink and gold clouds came and went, sprawling lazily across the sky, casting the entire world in a pale light. Yaara and Anne moved around easily, dropping their packs to the ground and digging out blankets, flints, and glass bottles of water.

When Yaara handed his bag to Knox, he could not hide his shock.

"Where did you get this?"

"Thought you might need it," she said. Relief crested over him. He clutched the bag to his chest.

"Here," Anne said, tossing a bundle of blankets at Knox.

Knox caught them, dropping his bag in his surprise. "What is this?"

"We're not going to let you sleep in the dirt," she said.

"I—thank you." Knox clutched them to his chest and took a step, then two, away from their bustling activity, trying not to draw attention to himself.

Cailean looked up sharply. "Where are you going?"

"Out of your way," Knox replied. "I don't… do you need me to…."

"Just stay where I can see you," Cailean said, and he tossed a canteen to Knox, who caught it, unscrewed the cap, then drank it down greedily.

"Thank you," he said again, wiping his mouth with the back of his hand.

Cailean sat back on his heels and narrowed his eyes. He held his flint in one hand, which he rested on his thigh. "You're welcome. Now shut up, I'm trying to start this fire."

"I can—" Knox began, but he stopped himself and bit his lip. "Never mind."

"No," Cailean said. "What can you do?"

"The fire," Knox said, nodding his head toward it. His heart swooped. What the hell was he doing? Cailean could probably rip his arm out of the socket, beat him to death with the bloody end of it, and not even break a sweat. "I can help."

"Can you," Cailean said flatly. He lifted his arm and held out his flint. "Go on, then."

Trembling, Knox stepped forward and looked down at the fire pit Cailean had arranged. The wood was too wet to burn, but it didn't matter, because no sooner had Knox looked at it and wished for it to burn than the flame was leaping into the air, reaching out for the darkening sky.

Cailean lifted his head slowly and met Knox's gaze. Knox's breath caught against his chest. He tore his gaze away, turned quickly, and dropped his blankets to the ground as Anne let out a low whistle.

"He never just used the Elements."

"He did," Yaara replied, and Knox would have liked to listen to the rest of their conversation, but he'd walked for miles and miles that day, and his body was weary. Without truly meaning to, he curled up in his blankets and was fast asleep before he heard another word.

It was dark when he woke. The skies were full to bursting with pinpricks of light, hovering closely overhead.

"You'll be wanting your dinner," Yaara said. She still had her hand on Knox's shoulder after having shaken him awake. "Are you hungry? You must be. We forgot to stop for lunch."

Knox rubbed the heels of his hands into his eyes. "What time's it?"

"No idea," Yaara said. "We don't really mark time as you do." She handed him a dented metal plate filled with delicious smoky meat and a handful of berries so brightly red that they shone even in the dim light of the moon and the fire. "Here."

"Tides," Knox said. His stomach rumbled. He took a tentative bite of the meat, then another.

Yaara sat down on the ground beside him, wrapping her arms around her knees. "Good?"

"Very," Knox replied. "Thank you." He pointed to the berries. "These aren't poisonous, are they?"

Yaara laughed and reached over. She took one of the berries from Knox's plate and popped it in her mouth. Then she grinned and opened her mouth, showing Knox the half-chewed berry on her tongue.

"That's… disgusting," he said. "And oddly reassuring."

"Quite," Yaara said. She waved her hands as though she'd done a party trick. Knox wished he did not find her endearing— bloodthirsty beasts weren't meant to be endearing, after all—but there was nothing for it. Perhaps it was simply the exhaustion and the hunger. With a full stomach and a good night's rest, he'd see everything more clearly.

He ate with very little ceremony, pulling the meat apart and shoving it into his mouth. His breakfast had been hours and hours ago, and after their long hike, he was starving. His fingers were slick and greasy in no time, and Knox stuck them in his mouth one by one, licking them clean.

"We weren't sure what you ate. Cailean does most of the hunting, so I'll let him know you inhaled the rabbit."

It occurred to Knox that aside from the fire, Yaara, and himself, the campsite was quiet and empty. "Where is he? Cailean?"

"He and Anne have gone to run," Yaara said, but she offered no further explanation and instead reached over and took another of the berries from Knox's plate.

For a few moments, they were quiet. Knox ate his dinner, and Yaara stared into the fire, opening and closing her mouth as if she wanted to speak. Her stillness was unnatural, her skin casting a heat warmer than any human's. Finally Knox could stand it no longer, and he pushed his plate away and asked, "Why are you doing this?"

"Cailean asked me to."

"Asked you to feed me?"

Yaara turned her head. "Feed you? No, I meant he asked me to keep an eye on you."

"Make sure I didn't run off."

"Make sure you were looked after."

Knox glanced at her. "So it's your job to take care of me after he kidnapped me."

She laughed. "Kidnapped you from your kidnappers? We did no such thing."

"Didn't you?" Knox asked, too tired and full to be careful. "I seem to remember arrows flying at me and a knife at my throat."

"They weren't our arrows."

"But it was Cailean's knife."

"We are not your enemy, Magus. We have no enemy but the Council, and it was the Council's arrow aimed at your chest. What is it you humans say? The enemy of my enemy is my friend?"

"That's—" Knox frowned. "The Council isn't my enemy."

She tilted her head like a bird. "Aren't they?"

"No," Knox said. His palms were sweating, and he had to wipe them on his trousers. "Of course not."

"Really?" she asked. "That's not what we hear."

"And how would you know anything about it?"

"We know plenty about everything," she said. "And we didn't kidnap you. Removing you from the Council was a favor."

"Right," Knox said, laughing in disbelief. "That makes complete sense. Being held against my will with razor sharp claws at my throat is a favor."

Yaara shrugged and tossed a stick into the fire. "Think what you like. But there's more you need to know before you make any decisions."

"Such as?"

"Cailean will speak with you."

Knox pushed his plate at Yaara and stood up, heaving a frustrated breath out at the night sky. "I'm honestly sick and bloody tired of other people deciding what information I should and should not have access to. Why don't you just tell me what it is you think I need to know and let me make up my own damn mind?"

Yaara arched an unimpressed eyebrow at him. "Are you quite done?"

"I'm going," Knox said, turning on his heels. Before he could take a single step, Yaara had him flat on his back with her knee digging into his stomach.

"I said, are you done?"

Knox nodded, his hair dragging in the dirt. Yaara's grip was tipped with sharp claws, and her eyes glowed fiercely.

"Good," she bit out. "Because you'll know… more than you could possibly want—in good time. But right now, it isn't my place to tell you. It's Cailean's."

"Because he's the prince."

Yaara shrugged and stood up, hauling Knox back to his feet. "For a number of reasons."

"Brilliant, but I'm looking around"—he waved his arms at the empty campsite—"and he isn't here."

"I am," Cailean said, coming into the clearing with Anne at his heels. He stood at least a full foot taller than Anne and shared her golden skin. His hair, so dark it was nearly blue, was pushed back from his forehead, and the curve of his collarbones gleamed in the light of the fire.

Knox crossed his arms over his chest and forced himself not to turn away, even though standing under the full weight of Cailean's attention was a blinding, staggering thing.

"We'll speak in the morning. Get some sleep," Cailean said. "Unless you can see in the dark, we leave at first light."

It was not first light when Knox woke, but it wasn't much past. Knox stirred from his bundle of blankets and found the fire had been tended in the night. He curled toward it, relishing the warmth on his face.

"Rise and shine, you great lump," Yaara said. "Word was sent for Cailean, and he and Anne had to go. We'll meet up with them in the next day or two. We're all headed in the same direction anyway."

Knox groaned and pushed his blanket down. "And where is that exactly?"

"Cairn. Where else?"

"When did they leave?"

"Hours ago."

Knox's eyes widened. "Hours? Did they sleep at all? And who sent word in the middle of the night in the middle of a great forest?"

Yaara rolled her eyes and handed Knox half a loaf of potato bread. "You're full of questions, aren't you? Go on, eat. We won't stop again for hours."

She broke their camp quickly and efficiently, so that by the time she was stuffing their blankets back into her pack, the land hardly looked disturbed. Even the fire ring was disposed of, the blackened stones scattered far and wide.

"Shall I carry that?" Knox asked, motioning for Yaara's pack.

Yaara grinned and tossed him the pack. It hit Knox in the chest, knocking an "oof" from him as he tumbled to the ground.

"You don't have to be a gentleman," she said. She walked over, took up the pack again, and swung it over her shoulders.

"What have you got in there?" Knox wheezed, staggering back to his feet.

"A bit of this, a bit of that," she replied, looping her arms through the straps. "Come on, then. No point in waiting for the sun to get any higher."

Yaara didn't move as quickly as Cailean, but she was still a beast and she set a grueling pace. Knox hustled into step beside her, entirely unsure of what to do with his hands. Eventually he shoved them into his pockets, then decided that felt stupid. He pulled them out again and let them swing by his sides, but that was even worse. He curled his hands into fists and wiped the sweat from his brow on the back of his sleeve. His mind raced as he moved around the puddles Yaara pointed out and jumped over the fallen trees that blocked their path. She carried no weapons, wore nothing that could be considered armor. Her bare skin was without blemish or mark.

"Do you remember what you said last night?" he asked finally, when he could stand the silence no longer. "About the enemy of my enemy?"

"As it was only yesterday evening, I believe so."

"You should know that they have my father. The Council, they have him. That's why I was…."

"We know that, Knox. That's the only reason you're not dead yet."

Knox could not begin to puzzle out what a comment like that meant. "How could you possibly know that?"

"There's very little we don't know. Dunmore, Greenfall, the whole lot." She glanced over her shoulder. "We see more than you could possibly imagine."

"How? How is that possible? I thought you all lived in the Cairn, way up into the northern mountains."

Yaara's grin was feral. "No," she said, showing him her teeth. "Very few of us do."

Knox took a deep breath and found that, for once, the truth came easy. "I don't trust you."

"I know," she replied easily. "Nor I you."

They met up with Cailean and Anne later that day on the outskirts of Norbough, nestled in the arms of a once great Old city. The miles they had traveled had been long, but the altitude they had gained made everything so much worse. It was cold, and the air was so thin Knox could hardly catch his breath. Knox had always thought Ailis a beautiful place, but the sameness of his hours was beginning to wear at him. The hours had lurched and lumbered by, filled with mile after mile of cumbersome terrain, this day very much the same as the ones he had spent with Cathal, Brae, and Pol. Every part of him ached, and his knees, ankles, and hips felt as though they were fitted together out of rusted bolts and broken glass. Between that and his sheer anxiety about his father's wellbeing, Knox was surprised he hadn't broken out into hives yet.

He was sweaty, dirty, and exhausted and longed for a bath so badly he considered trying his luck with the Elements again, just to see if he could conjure up a spring or a pond. Or hell, even a large puddle would have been welcome. It did not even matter that the days were cooling rapidly and the previous night had been near freezing. If someone had handed Knox an ice block, he'd have considered it a luxury.

Knox's mind ran over with questions that wanted answers. He had them stored up like grain for a coming winter to the point where everything in his head felt thick and fuzzy, so he hardly even noticed that Cailean and Anne were there at the edge of Norbough. One moment he was watching his footfalls in the hard-packed dirt. The next, he was leaning on Anne as Yaara and Cailean muttered furiously at one another.

"How the hell did you beat us here?" Cailean was asking, Yaara's arm caught in his bruising grip. "There's no way you should have—Yaara, look at him. He's half-dead on his feet."

Knox wanted to protest, but the truth was he felt quite a bit more than half-dead on his feet, and the support Anne was giving him was the most glorious thing he'd known in days. He leaned into her further, letting the warmth of her shoulder ease the chill spread through his chest.

"You'd have preferred we took the scenic route?" Yaara asked, glaring at Cailean. "What, you thought we'd have an amble through the countryside? You told me to get him—"

"Alive," Cailean said. "I said for you to get him here alive. He can't even stand, Yaara."

"I can stand," Knox said, though the words slurred coming out of his mouth. "I'm fine. I may not be a beast, but I can walk, can't I?"

The silence that fell on them was absolute, stark and blank like a blanket of rock. It rang in Knox's ears as clearly as a bell. He looked up from Anne's shoulder to find Cailean and Yaara staring at him. Their faces were contorting with fury, turning each of them into something animalistic and terrifying. Knox tried to straighten, but without Anne to support him—for she was staring as well, every muscle in her body whipcord tight and ready to strike—he stumbled and nearly went down to one knee.

"What—" Cailean spat out. He took in a deep breath, his nostrils flaring. "What did you just say?"

Knox shook his head and forced his lungs to work. "I said I can walk. I'm not a cripple."

"Before that," Cailean said, and his claws slid out a fraction, then back in. Knox forced his head up, forced himself to meet Cailean's gaze, overcome with an absolute certainty he was about to die, for he had seen anger and he had seen rage, and neither of them was even close to the cold and savage wrath drawn in every line of Cailean's body.

He found it almost a relief, really, weary and ragged and defeated as he was. He was only sorry he would never see his father again, would never apologize for everything his magic had cost them. He shut his eyes and swayed on his feet.

"What did you say, human?"

"I...." Knox forced his dry throat to work. "I don't know what you mean."

"What did you call us?" Cailean demanded.

Knox pushed aside the cobwebs crowding his brain and tried to recall his words. "Beasts?" he said at length, and that must have been it, because Anne hissed in a breath and Cailean let out a low growl that shook Knox's bones. With difficulty, he looked over at Yaara, who, while certainly not a friend, was the closest thing to it he had in the unfathomable situation he found himself in. But Yaara was looking at him with murder in her sharp eyes.

"Never say that word," she spat out, her face contorted in anger. "We're not beasts. We're not *animals*. It's you," she went on, pointing a shaking hand at Knox. "Your lot are the animals. It's you humans who—"

"Yaara," Anne said. She moved between them, but the taut line of her body betrayed her words. "He doesn't know. How could he? Stupid humans, they don't know anything. Would you kill him for his ignorance?"

"They killed us over their own."

"I didn't—please," Knox said. His head spun, and he staggered. "I don't understand."

"You call us beasts," Cailean said, drawing himself up to his full height. His chest was broad, his shoulders powerful and so mighty Knox found himself captivated by them. "But we are not animals. We are not beasts. We are *wolves*." The word was weighted with so much pride, Knox felt a tremor race up his back. It seemed the earth would break under his feet. "Noble and strong, and loyal to our pack in a way you humans"—he spat the word like a curse—"could never know. We are *Mac Tire*. We are the sons of the countryside."

"Mac Tire," Knox said. He forced the cold, biting air into his lungs and made himself look at each of them in turn. Yaara, with her strong shoulders and shifting muscles. Anne, with her flashing eyes that caught the light and seemed to hold as much magic as Knox had ever dreamed of commanding. And Cailean, whose very voice made Knox's heart shake. "I've heard that word. The first night I saw you."

Yaara gasped and turned, glaring at Knox so fiercely he took a step back.

"What?" she whispered flatly. "What did you say? Where did you hear that?"

"The pub," Knox said. "In Dunmore. The barkeep, Duff? I asked who Cailean was, and he called him Mac Tire."

If it was possible, Yaara's face tightened even further. She whipped around and stared at Cailean, but whatever was causing her fury, Cailean did not seem to recognize it.

"Why did you ask about me?" he demanded.

"I—I don't know," Knox said, holding his frozen fingers up in front of himself. They were a bloodless white. That couldn't be good. "Something about you struck me. I asked the barkeep and he told me your name. He called you Mac Tire."

"Who were you with?" Yaara asked, grabbing Cailean's arm. "Cailean, were you with Jarlath?"

"You were gathering information on me for the Council," Cailean said. "Did you tell the others about me?" He shook off

Yaara's grip and advanced on Knox, grabbing him by the collar of his shirt and pulling him nearly off his feet. "Answer me!"

"No!" Knox shouted. "No, I told no one. I went back, I… stole their maps, memorized them."

"Maps?" Cailean cocked his head to the side. "What maps?"

"There were two. Sightings," Knox said. "Of be—of you. Of those like you. And another that showed the boundaries of the city, the main towers of the ráth."

Anne rumbled something into Cailean's ear, and even Yaara left off her attempts at getting Cailean's attention to let out something like a growl.

"Do you have these maps now? I demand you give them to me at once."

"I had to put them back," Knox said. "Otherwise they'd know it was me who took them. But I stole a sheet of paper when I was writing a missive to the Council—"

Cailean's grip went tighter still. Knox could scarcely touch the ground with the tips of his boots. "What did you write to the Council?"

"Nothing," he gasped out. "Nothing. Lies. Brae wanted me to say we were making progress, but we weren't. No one had any information. Or none they would give up, it seems."

"Yaara," Cailean said, releasing Knox, who staggered and wrapped his arms around his stomach, his head swimming. "Go to Dunmore, you and Anne. Check that Jarlath is safe, that we have not been betrayed."

He glared at Knox as he said this, as if Knox had any loyalty to the beasts. He had no loyalty to anyone except his father.

"Bring us word as quickly as you can. We must move. It is time."

"Thank you, Sire," Yaara breathed, the first mention or even nod toward Cailean's reign. "Thank you." She stepped up to Cailean and rubbed her cheek on his. He touched her hand.

"I pray you success."

Yaara stepped back, and Anne took her place, pushing up on her toes to rub her cheek against Cailean's. "Be wise," she told him. Cailean touched her head.

"I pray you safe travel."

And with that, they were gone, swallowed up by the forest. Cailean turned and met Knox's gaze, nodding once. "You better be telling the truth."

"I don't care about the Council. All I care about is getting my father back."

"If that is true, you have nothing to fear from us." He set his mouth, grabbed Knox's arm, and propelled him forward. Little more than a dead weight, Knox let himself be pushed.

The settlement was smaller than any of the others Knox had come through. Most of the Old buildings had long ago been lost to weather and time, and all that remained of them were the flat squares of concrete that had once been their foundations. The new houses were in rows of three or four, their walls pressed together to keep the heat in. Most were already shut up against the evening's cold when Knox and Cailean came through, their doors pulled tight against the wind, their windows covered with bits of paper and cloth.

Knox was starving, but too tired and cold to do anything about his hunger. It gnawed at him in an empty way, made him stumble from weakness. He didn't even have the energy to be embarrassed.

"This is madness," Cailean muttered. He loosened his grip on Knox's elbow and steered him away from the shop and toward one of the small homes that lined the streets. "Come with me."

Lacking both the ability to pull away and the desire to argue, Knox let Cailean pull him along, stumbling and sliding in the icy slush that lined the streets. Eventually, they came to a tiny, A-frame house that was dim inside, but something about it made a spark alight in Knox's chest, warming him from within. He lifted his head as Cailean swung the door open. The warmth of the small home was as solid as a wall. Knox could have wept in relief.

Cailean stepped quickly inside, dragging Knox after him. The woman who had opened the door gasped and grabbed Cailean, pulling him to her chest. "Cailean? It's been days! We thought—"

"I've had word," Cailean cut in, wrapping his arms around the woman and touching her cheek. "He's safe. He's across the ráth."

They stood for several long minutes, holding on to one another in the quiet of the small sitting room. Knox stood by awkwardly, inching toward the fire that flickered and leapt in the hearth.

"Will he meet you here? Or will you go to him?" the woman asked. She was beautiful, with warm olive skin and dark hair that hung down her back. She nearly reached Cailean's head in height. "Is he prepared to move forward?"

"I'm not sure. We need to speak together and decide the best way to proceed. Things have grown complicated. Yaara and Anne had to return to Dunmore to fetch Jarlath. And I've—" He paused and looked over at Knox, who was nearly curled around the fire, his hands stretched out toward the flame. Cailean bit his lip and met the eyes of the woman, who glanced at Knox, then startled as if she had not realized there was a second person in her sitting room. "I've taken the Magus from the Council's men."

The woman raised her eyebrows. "Taken?" she said. "You mean rescued."

Cailean sighed. "I'm not quite sure he sees it that way."

"Oh, Cailean," she said, sighing and sinking down onto the threadbare couch. "What have you done now?"

Cailean dropped his things to the floor and whirled around, fixing his flashing gaze on the woman. To her credit, she did not flinch or even blink. "They intended to use him against us, Rhys."

"And you've secured his loyalty by kidnapping him and dragging him halfway across Ailis."

"I haven't kidnapped anyone," Cailean bit out. "That's the Council's work, not mine."

She fixed him with a stern glare. "So the boy is free to go, is he?"

An appearance of tiredness came over Cailean then, and he slumped forward, leaning his weight against the wall and dropping his head into his hands. He rubbed the heels of his hands into his eyes and sighed. "Rhys."

"You're so reckless," she said, touching his wrist. "Have you eaten?"

Cailean shook his head. "You should see to the Magus. He's been traveling with Yaara, who paid his limitations no mind. He's likely starved, half-dead, and lucky if all his toes are still attached."

"I don't need looking after," Knox cut in, drawing himself up, trying to look formidable but unwilling to move too far away from the fire. "I'm called Knox, not Magus or boy, and all my toes are fine, thank you. And I can hunt my own food."

The woman—Rhys—grinned at him, showing the same slightly pointed teeth as Cailean. "Not half-dead, then, are you?"

Knox met her gaze, refusing to falter. It rankled, being spoken of so. He'd have given an arm for a warm meal, but here, in a cabin with two unknown beasts, any sign of weakness was unacceptable. "No."

"That's admirable, Magus, but you'll have a time finding game this far north, especially at this time of evening. Everything with any sense is bedded down. But there's salted ham and fresh pottage in the kitchen, and ale to help warm you. Cailean will bring in some wood."

"I can fetch my own wood," Knox said.

It was no small feat, but Knox managed to load up his arms with the split logs that were stacked neatly beside the rear door. He carried them back inside under the watchful eye of Cailean, who stood in the open doorway, back to the door, thick arms crossed over his chest. He glared at Knox with his brow drawn into a deep furrow.

"What?" he asked, dumping the wood inside the doorway. Cailean said nothing, just turned and stepped into what Knox assumed was the kitchen. By the time he returned with a chipped bowl of steaming pottage, Knox had insinuated himself in front of the hearth again, where the heat was finally beginning to seep into his bones. He accepted the bowl with a nod.

Cailean returned to the kitchen and began speaking in hushed tones with Rhys.

Knox didn't even try to listen in; his body was so exhausted it had nearly ceased to operate upright. A few moments later, Rhys and Cailean came back into the small, shabbily outfitted sitting room.

"There is little we can do tonight," Cailean said. "You should sleep, Magus."

Nothing sounded better to Knox. He would have happily curled up on the hearth, baking in the heat like a cat if they'd only leave him be. It was no worse than the ground. At least tonight's bed would be indoors.

"Knox, I believe it is," Rhys said. She raised her eyebrows at Cailean, then nodded at Knox. "If we expect him to give us our due respect, we should at least afford him the same courtesy."

Surprised at her kindness, Knox nodded back, swallowing around the lump in his throat. "Mac Tire," he murmured, too tired to care if the address was properly done, or even adequate. Now that he had a warm fire and a full belly, it was all Knox could do to stay upright. As it was, he found himself listing toward the wall and subsequently the floor. But a smile spread quickly across Rhys's face, and she tilted her chin toward Knox. Cailean, if he heard Knox, gave no notice. He touched his hand to the small of Rhys's back, face as impassive as ever.

"Cailean," Rhys said, placing her hand on Cailean's forearm and leaning in to touch her cheek against his. Cailean's eyes drifted shut; the stubble on his cheek caught at the long hairs trailing over her shoulders.

"I pray you safe travel," Cailean said. "And swift feet."

"One of those I can assure you," she replied. Then with another touch to Cailean's arm, she left the cabin so quickly she might have been snatched from it by some unseen force, leaving behind only the chill that swept in after the door snapped shut behind her. Knox blinked at the air she'd left behind.

"Here," Cailean said, and he tossed a bundle of blankets and quilts at Knox. Knox caught them easily.

"What's this?"

"You want to sleep on the hard floor?"

"Not really, no."

"All right, then."

"Where's she gone?" Knox found himself asking, not especially keen to be left alone with Cailean. Yesterday he'd been nearly overcome with questions for the beast, but now, alone with him and worn down to the quick, all he wanted was safety and a night of bloody sleep.

"Mind your own business," Cailean snapped.

When he was younger and quick to lose his temper, Knox's father would ask him "Is this your breaking point?" and Knox would always calm himself, because then Uilleam would tell him, "No, this is not the point when you break. You must never break, Knox. You must never, ever break. When you break is when your secrets become known." With his father's voice in his ears, Knox knelt on the floor and made a soft pallet from the blankets Cailean had given him. He arranged them as near to the fire as he dared, then lay down and fell asleep before he could concern himself further with Cailean, Rhys, Yaara, and Anne and this whole mad journey.

SIX

WHEN KNOX woke, it took him several long moments to become fully aware of his surroundings. It faded in slowly, the darkness giving way to deep grays and golden yellows, the space around him coming into fullness and light. Knox rubbed his eyes, then looked around, mildly surprised to find himself not on the floor as he had been when he fell asleep but sprawled across a low-to-the-ground bed that fit underneath a deeply sloping ceiling.

Looking around, Knox saw that the room held very little furniture apart from the bed. A dented old cupboard, a rickety chair that stood beside the bed, and across from that, an old trunk upon which rested a folded stack of faded quilts.

Knox stretched carefully, wincing at the pull in his muscles. His back ached, and one shoulder felt as though it had been sacrificed for someone's pound of flesh, but his legs had lost that ache that had bewitched him these last few days. It was, all in all, not a terrible waking up, and even better when Knox looked over at the chair and noticed a cup of steaming liquid. He grabbed it and bent his neck over the cup, breathing in earthy scent. Careful not to slosh it on the bed, he took a deep sip, then another. The tea, if that's what it was, was unlike any Knox had ever had. It was rich and bitter, warming Knox through to the marrow. Before long, the cup was empty, and Knox pushed the covers aside and stood up.

His pack was tucked underneath the chair. Knox grabbed it and dug inside, coming up with a washing cloth and a spare set of clothes. He dug his hand down to the bottom of the pack, breathing a sigh of relief when his fingers closed over the spare sheet of paper he'd smuggled away from Cathal.

Knox tossed the clothes on the bed, then closed the pack and stowed it under the chair again. He found a basin of freezing water on top of the cupboard. He dunked his cloth into it, gasped at the chill, then washed as quickly as possible, shifting his weight from foot to foot. Then, drawn out by his hunger, he opened the door to the room and nearly toppled down the steel flight of stairs directly in front of him.

"Tides!" he shouted, grappling for the handrail. He nearly caught it; his fingers brushed the edge of it as he crashed downward, tumbling ass-first to the sitting room below.

He came to a stop all at once, his feet resting on the wall above him. Smarting everywhere, Knox closed his eyes. "No one saw," he muttered. "No one is in the house."

He opened his eyes and found Cailean staring at him from across the room, holding a large blue mixing bowl in one hand and a wooden spoon in the other.

"Oh," he said. "Um."

Cailean turned on his heel and walked back into the kitchen. "It's midday."

"Oh," Knox said. "Sorry."

"No, don't be. I expected you to sleep much longer to be honest. Even the strongest humans have trouble keeping pace with us."

"Right, well, then." Cailean's words were like a pail of cold water to the face. Knox wasn't sure why he'd expected any better. He brushed his hands off on his pants as he staggered to his feet. "I beg your forgiveness for my weaker nature."

Knox followed Cailean into the kitchen, then hovered in the doorway watching as Cailean's big hands made quick work of the dough on the counter. It was a hypnotic thing, watching him work: the flex of his wrists, the way he turned and flipped the dough. His face was impassive, and only the set of his broad shoulders betrayed the tension that sat on top of them.

"Whose house is this?"

"Are you hungry? You must be."

"You all think me so feeble."

"I'm the one who dragged your half-dead body upstairs last night after you collapsed on the floor. I wouldn't think a bit of gratitude would go amiss, though expecting it from your lot is a futile pursuit, is it not?"

"I don't know what you mean when you say *my lot*."

"Humans," Cailean said. He spat out the word as though it was a foul-tasting thing.

"I wonder why you'd take the trouble then to haul me upstairs and feed me," Knox said, "when you find my mere existence so distasteful."

"Well these are odd times, aren't they?" said Cailean. He covered the dough and left it to rise, then brushed past Knox on his way up the small staircase that led to the tiny attic where Knox had slept. And Knox followed him without really meaning to, because though he had been asleep in Cailean's care for any number of hours, now that he was awake, the idea of the beast being alone with the few possessions Knox had stowed away in his bag was untenable. He scampered quickly up the stairs, burst into the room, and found Cailean doing nothing more suspicious than gathering up the cup beside the bed and turning to go.

"Back to sleep already?" Cailean said. "Would you like some warm milk, or a bedtime story?"

"I'm simply getting my things," Knox said, scowling. "I thought I might try to recreate that map I saw."

"You might be useful yet," Cailean said. He turned sideways to slip past Knox to go down the steps. He was so broad and the doorway so small that, as they passed, it seemed an endless number of places on them brushed together, and every place they touched burned.

Knox took a moment to gather himself, then he took up his bag and went back downstairs. Only once he had fetched the bit of paper and spread it out before him on the narrow, low-to-the-ground table in the kitchen did Knox realize his predicament: while he had paper, he had no pencil or quill or truly anything with which to write, and judging by the smirk upon his handsome face, Cailean knew just that. It was irritating, being read so easily by someone who knew him so little.

Knox smoothed the creases out of the paper again and again as Cailean bustled around the kitchen with a smug look that Knox wanted to knock clean off his face. And in the same way it was clear that Cailean knew he had no pencil, it was clear that Cailean would not offer one. With little choice, Knox pushed himself to his feet and began wandering around the room, looking on shelves and in drawers, seeking anything with which to write.

Cailean was on him in a flash. "What do you think you're doing?"

"I'm looking for a pencil," Knox said calmly.

Cailean's eyes flashed and burned. The hand on Knox's arm tightened, and Knox knew he should feel threatened. He knew he should be shaking, and he knew he should be terrified, but for some reason... he was none of those things. Something in Knox, some bit of magic, sparked and skittered up and down his spine, unfurled beneath his skin, stretched toward his fingertips.

He blinked slowly and dragged his eyes up to look at Cailean.

"This," Cailean said, releasing Knox's arm and stepping back, "is my sister's house, and you will treat it with respect."

"Your sister?" Knox said. "You have a sister? I thought...."

"You don't know anything about me," Cailean said. He fell back a step and then another. It was only one more step across the kitchen. Cailean reached over and plucked a pencil off a shelf. It was a small nub of a thing; their fingers brushed when Cailean handed it to him.

Knox sat down at the table, unable to pull his gaze from Cailean's profile.

"Well, are you drawing the map or aren't you?" Cailean burst out a moment later. "Fuck, bloody humans. I'm going to get firewood." The door slammed shut behind him, leaving Knox quite alone.

It took him the better part of the day to sketch out the map. He filled in as much detail as he could remember. He tried to draw it to scale so it would be of some use to them—no, to *him* when he had to cross the ráth to get to his father. He marked each place where the ráth was fortified, marked each place where it would be vulnerable. Then he folded the map, tucked it away in his bag, took the bit of pencil and placed it back on the counter, and sat down in front of the fire to wait.

As he waited, Knox's mind turned to his father. If Brae and the others were returning to the city to report Knox's capture to the Council, Knox's father could be in even greater danger. He needed to figure out how to get back to the city, and soon. For a brief moment, he considered grabbing his pack and making a run for it, but Cailean was just outside, and Yaara had already shown Knox exactly what was thought of his feeble attempts at escape.

If, however, Brae and the others had decided against returning to the citadel—and this, Knox thought, was the more likely case, seeing as they had not seemed at all keen for the Council to doubt the inevitably of their success—time was on Knox's side. He just had to figure out what the beasts—no, *wolves*—wanted from him. So far, they'd requested nothing of him, though Cailean had hinted that he would take possession of Knox's map without a second thought. Knox had always valued his patience, hard-fought as it had been for his father to drill it into him, but exhaustion and fear were getting the better of him. No man could be expected to wait forever.

The heat of the fire kept the house almost too warm. There wasn't much to it: a small, shabbily outfitted sitting room, which opened into an even smaller kitchen. The two spaces were separated by nothing more than a squat bookshelf that was built into the wall and covered with neatly bound volumes. Above Knox was the tiny attic, and that seemed the end of it.

Was this the way all wolves lived? Hidden away in the settlements? For a long time, Knox had believed they'd been separated from the rest of Ailis by the nearly impassable northern mountains, but clearly, that wasn't anything that bordered on truth. Knox found he wasn't sure what to believe anymore. Everything was upside down and inside out.

When Cailean came back in, his face was flushed pink and his breath was high in his chest, as though he had just run a great distance. Knox watched out of the corner of his eye as Cailean moved into the kitchen and uncovered the dough he'd left rising on the counter. He placed it upon a large, flat stone, which he slipped into the wood-burning stove that dominated the small kitchen.

Cailean stood up and stretched, rolled his neck from side to side. The muscles under his golden skin shifted and bunched, and truly, it was unfair of him to be so bloody attractive and such a complete jerk all at once. In another world, Knox might have enjoyed looking at Cailean. In this one, the sight of that stubbornly set jaw and stoic face made Knox want to scream.

"You finished the map?"

Knox jerked, his face heating up when he realized Cailean must have caught him staring.

"What?" he croaked.

"The map," Cailean repeated. He seemed focused on the stove, had not even lifted his head to look at Knox. Knox's breath left him in a great whoosh. "You finished it?"

"Um, yes."

Cailean stepped closer, holding out a hand. Knox wondered if he recognized the scope of himself—the weight of his presence. "Let's have it, then."

"Sorry," Knox said, shrinking back, but holding the map to his chest all the same. "What?"

"You want to be useful, then make yourself useful. Hand it over."

"I don't want to be useful," Knox said. "I'd like to go and find my father."

"You're toying with things beyond your understanding, Magus. Just—" Cailean reached down and wrenched the map out of Knox's grip. Rather than risk ripping it, Knox loosened his grip and let Cailean take it. Any protest he might have given voice to died on Knox's lips at the hungry way Cailean raked his gaze over the map, and his heart clenched. The dead space in Cailean's eyes was replaced with a spark that Knox could clearly see, even in the fading light of evening.

"*Forradh*," Cailean murmured, touching the map with his fingertip. "*Lia Fáil*."

He closed his eyes and tightened his grip on the paper. His words were a prayer. Knox's face burned, and he looked away.

Cailean stared at it for another long moment, then handed the map back. The side of it was creased from Cailean's grip. Knox placed it on his thigh and smoothed it.

"How much longer do you intend to keep me here?"

"What would you do if you left?" Cailean asked. "You've no provisions, no money. You'd be dead in three days, if you even lasted that long. You'd likely freeze to death before you figured out which way was south."

"I need to get to Cahircluain. My father—"

"You're going to rescue him yourself, are you? How exactly do you intend to go about that? You're going to take on a whole city worth of the Council's soldiers?"

"I have magic," Knox said stubbornly.

Cailean dragged his hands over his face. "I honor your loyalty, Magus, I do. If it's genuine—"

"He's my *father*. He's the only thing in this world I am loyal to."

Cailean looked at him, his eyes piercing. The fire had not gone out of them. "Not the Council?"

"They're the ones who have him!" Knox burst out. Fury overtook him, and his chest heaved and words tumbled out of his mouth. "They beat him, they locked him away so that I'd kill you, you great bloody beast. Why the fuck would I have any loyalty to them?"

"Why haven't you?"

"Why haven't I what?" Knox demanded. It took him a moment to realize he was staring right up into Cailean's face. He had crossed the room without even realizing it and was inches from Cailean. The heat of his body was like a brick wall against Knox's chest.

"Killed me," Cailean said. Then he quirked an eyebrow. "Or tried to, at least."

Knox's mouth fell open, but no words came. What could he possibly say? That some spark of his magic kept him from even considering the idea? That he trusted him, without even understanding why? It sounded mad, even to Knox.

He shut his mouth and took a step back.

"It's getting late," Cailean finally said, when the tension had stretched out so far Knox thought it would snap back and slap him in the face. "Are you hungry?"

Knox was. He took the bread and dried meat Cailean offered him, and they ate in silence. Finally, when their plates were empty and their bellies full, Cailean said, "You should get some sleep. We'll talk more tomorrow."

"I seem to remember you telling me that days ago and"—he spread his arms out wide—"here we are."

Cailean sighed, his shoulders sagging. "Just... go to bed, Magus."

Knox bristled. He hated how affected he was by this... this beast.

"Look," he began, but Cailean turned and walked back into the kitchen. The space was so small that he couldn't have been more than twelve feet away, but Knox was damned if he was going to shout at the arrogant jerk's back. He pushed himself to his feet and turned to the steps, but couldn't stop himself from firing one parting shot. "My patience is wearing thin, Cailean."

"Believe it or not, human, on that score you and I are in complete accord."

FOR ALL of his assurances, nothing was clearer the next morning. Knox rose shortly after dawn, when the twittering of birds in the trees outside his window grew too loud for him to ignore. He straightened the covers on his bed and went downstairs to find Cailean already awake and outside, shirtless and sweating as he took himself through a series of exercises. He paused when Knox came outside, grunted a greeting, then returned to his pull-ups.

There was no reason for Knox's face to turn so hot at the sight of Cailean gleaming and sweating in the weak morning sunlight. Knox had seen shirtless men before, too many of them to count, but certainly none as beautiful as Cailean. The way Cailean affected him was mortifying. Knox's face burned to see the breadth of Cailean's shoulders, the span of his chest, and the taper of his waist beneath his pants.

Perhaps he needed to acclimate himself to it. All the beasts—no, the Mac Tire—were as beautiful as Cailean. Anne and Yaara were both stunning in their own right. Of course neither of them made Knox's heart stir, but examining that would do no good, so Knox pushed the thought from his head and sat down on the ground to let himself get accustomed to Cailean's beauty. He crossed his arms and propped them on his knees, staring off into the woods with Cailean in his periphery. Smart not to overwhelm himself with too much of Cailean's skin all at once.

The trees vibrated with life. Knox opened up his magic and let it wander through the forest. There was very little large game, but there were foxes and boar aplenty. And more birds than Knox could count. The trees were alive with them, and their songs whipped together into a symphony. Knox emptied his head of everything else and listened to them, trying to distinguish their songs from one another. It was unlike anything he'd ever heard. He began to pull at their threads, counting each one, and got as far as twenty-seven before Cailean grunted and dropped from the tree he'd been climbing, coming to rest in a crouch in front of Knox.

"Would you *stop* that?"

Knox startled. "Stop what?"

"Whatever it is you're doing with the birds. They're going crazy out there."

"You can sense that?"

Cailean glared. "It's deafening. I can't even hear myself think."

"Tides. No one has ever done that before."

"Yeah. Well." Cailean reached for his discarded shirt and wiped the sweat from his face. Knox looked away quickly.

"So, um. Can we have that conversation now?"

Cailean grunted and pulled his sweaty shirt over his head. It should have been disgusting. "Tomorrow. We'll talk tomorrow."

"We'll talk tomorrow? So what, we'll just spend all of today in silence?"

"Enjoyable as that would be, I doubt any human could manage it, you least of all."

"Excuse me? What do you mean me least of all?"

"Just that you seem to exist for the sole purpose of driving me insane," Cailean said, brushing past Knox and into the house. Knox followed him furiously.

"I exist for reasons that have absolutely nothing to do with you," Knox snapped. "But if annoying you is one of them, well." He spread his arms out wide. "Lucky me."

Cailean didn't answer, which annoyed Knox even more. He walked over to the basin and lifted it out of the cradle where it rested.

"What are you doing?"

Cailean rolled his eyes. "Going to get water to wash. If that's all right with you?"

Knox meant to make some sort of smart retort—what was it about this man that got under his skin and drove him to such distraction?—to tell Cailean that was fine with him because he reeked of sweat, but the fact was that he smelled wonderful to Knox. He smelled of earth, sunlight, and every good and golden thing Knox had always loved. He crossed his arms over his chest instead and hoped his face wasn't as red as it felt.

Cailean crossed the room, pausing at the doorway. "Seventeen seconds, by the way."

"What?"

"Seventeen seconds," Cailean repeated. "That's how long you lasted without talking."

"I—I…." Knox spluttered. "I didn't know we'd started!"

Cailean's laugh rang in Knox's ears for hours.

KNOX MADE a deal with himself. He wouldn't speak until Cailean spoke to him. He wouldn't make observations or ask questions. He wouldn't ask where Rhys had gone or when she was coming back.

He wouldn't question Cailean on his plan or demand to know when he would be allowed to leave. He wouldn't say anything at all. Unfortunately, Cailean caught on to his plan and, if the smile tugging at his lips all morning was any indication, found it far more amusing than Knox cared for. He took to peering at Knox from across the room with his eyebrows raised, as if he were waiting for Knox to break and ask a question.

Eventually, Knox couldn't hold it in any longer. "What did you mean when you said humans don't know how to be quiet? Is your lot—what do you call it? Mac Tire? Are you all so good at silence?"

Cailean shrugged and settled back into the couch with a satisfied look on his face. "We're more used to it. Most of my people live in solitude, having very little contact with the rest of the Mac Tire. It's just the way of things."

"Why is that? Why are you separated so? I thought you all were banished to Cairn?"

Cailean huffed a humorless laugh. "Banished," he echoed. "Banished from our own land. No, human. We do not accept the rule of your Council—"

"They're not *my* Council—"

"—because it is unjust. We are everywhere. It's easily done. No one opens their eyes. No one cares to see. For years now we've been spreading out through Ailis, positioning ourselves, simply waiting for the right time to act."

Knox's chest tightened. "And that time is now?"

Suddenly, Cailean froze. He tilted his head to one side, like a curious child, then moved quickly to the door and threw it open. "Rhys?

"It's us" came a female voice. A moment later, the two people came stumbling through the doorway. A tangle of dark hair that was clearly Rhys came first, and behind her she towed... Knox's head spun... it couldn't be....

"Uilleam," Cailean said formally, and Knox's father made a cursory bow toward him, then turned, his eyes finding Knox instantly.

"Knox," he said gruffly, and Knox crossed the room in two strides, flinging himself face first into his father's chest. He took a wet breath, unable to convince himself that this was real, that Uilleam was honestly here and was, as far as Knox could tell, whole and relatively unharmed.

"What," he said into his father's shoulder, unable to draw back long enough to speak, "what happened? Are you all right? Tides, Father...."

"I'm fine," Uilleam said, rubbing his hands in broad sweeping motions over Knox's back. "Knox, I'm fine. Look." He tried to push Knox away from him, but Knox shook his head and drew in a shuddering breath.

"I can't, just...."

Uilleam laughed softly. "I missed you too, son."

"I thought you were—they said they would—"

"There is very little the Council can do to me that has not been done before," Uilleam said, finally managing to untangle the pair of them. Knox let himself be drawn back so he could scan his father's face. The bruises under his eyes had yellowed with time, but the gash on his face was as ugly as it had been when Knox had been removed from him. His skin looked paper thin and pale, stretched over his bones. Knox had been born late in his father's life, a fact he'd never fully realized until that moment. "The worst they could manage was taking you from me. But I knew you were stronger than to let a few of their men get the better of you. Still," he went on, running his hand over Knox's hair. "I could not rest until word came that Cailean had found you."

"Cailean." Knox spun around but found the cottage empty. "Cailean, Father, he's... he's a beast." Uilleam's eyes widened, and Knox hastened to add, "I mean, that is to say, Mac Tire, they called themselves. This is his home."

"Knox," Uilleam said. "There is much to discuss, and we have so little time."

Knox's thoughts were slow, weighed down by exhaustion and confusion and the sheer, overwhelming fact of having his father back. When he'd been taken from Darry, Knox hardly dared believe they'd ever meet again, this side of heaven. What he wouldn't have given for a quiet room—with his father nearby—and a week to untangle the last several days in his head. It was what he'd always done when the magic in his chest got to be too much to handle: taken a deep breath, then another, and another and another until he was able to find the end of one string and work it free from the knot. A bit of that magic to clear up all of this wouldn't go amiss.

The sunlight coming in through the windows was pale and pink. It cast the room in a soft glow, but beyond that, the bitter wind howled, rattling the windows in their panes. He pressed the heels of his hands into his eyes until color burst behind his eyelids like exploding stars.

"How ever did you escape? The Council can't have let you go."

"One of Cailean's men came for me, mere hours after you left with the soldiers."

"How was he able to even enter the city? And how on earth did he manage to cross the Magus ráth?"

"The Council has grown foolish," Uilleam sighed. "Even more so than when they took the citadel years ago. Power has filled them to overflowing with their own importance. Always underestimating all the right people and overestimating all the wrong ones."

"I don't understand. Oh tides, but I hardly care. Are you well? Did they hurt you? I swear if they did—"

"Knox," Uilleam said, holding up a hand. His smile was soft and fond, but his eyes were weary.

"There is a conversation we are long overdue for. I wish... I'd hoped to keep you from this for longer," he said. "You're still so young, but.... I guess the arrow's off the bow now, isn't it? Come, Cailean and Rhys have likely gone to fetch dinner and give us some privacy to say our hellos."

"You know their names," Knox said wonderingly, still staring at his father's face as though he was a trick of the light, like seeing a skeleton in the dark that turns out to be a rake sat upon a stack of twigs in the daylight. Knox was terrified Uilleam would disappear if he so much as blinked.

"Come," Uilleam said. "Sit. I hardly know where to begin."

They settled into the couch. Knox drew a blanket from the back of it and settled it over Uilleam's legs. "Father, please."

Uilleam sighed and dragged his hands over his face. "Would a cup of tea go amiss?"

Knox arched his eyebrows, and Uilleam sighed again. "All right," Uilleam said. "All right. What do you know of the time when The Council came to power?"

Knox could not help the gasp of surprise that escaped him. They were starting from the very beginning, it seemed. "Very little, I expect. I know that the beasts ruled for centuries, that the settlements ruled themselves and paid tribute to the kingdom for protection. I know some twenty years there was a revolt and—"

"It wasn't a revolt," Uilleam interrupted. "It was an unmitigated slaughter. The Mac Tire were—they never saw it coming. Thousands of men were killed, women, children. Struck down indiscriminately. The Mac Tire had never sought to reign over or control the people. It's not their way; it never has been. They've always ruled their own kind with an unyielding strength—they had to with that sort of power—but they were *just*. Why do you think Cailean still commands them all, far flung as they are? They're everywhere, Knox. Not in the north. Not here in the mountains. They've been placing themselves strategically these past twenty years. The Resistance is rising, and they know Cailean will be a fair ruler, and that he'll return the city to them. Or he'll die trying. Theirs is a loyalty you cannot imagine, Knox."

"Uilleam."

Knox looked up and found Cailean standing in the doorway again, mouth pinched into a straight line.

"Cailean," Uilleam said. He stood up and laughed a bit breathlessly, shaking his head. "Or is it—I'm sorry, I don't quite know how to address you. I've not seen you since you were a teenager."

"Cailean is fine." He cleared his throat, scrubbing his palms on the thighs of his pants. "There is no place for formal addresses in circumstances such as this."

79

"Still," Uilleam began, but Cailean shook his head and held up a hand. Knox watched in fascination.

"I won't stand on ceremony here."

"Cailean, then," Uilleam said. "I owe you a great debt. Thank you for my son."

"Hang on," Knox cut in, because he wasn't at all sure being held captive by a terrifying beast was the same thing as being saved by one.

"It had to be done, Knox," Uilleam said. "I know you can't have liked the way it was handled, but there was no other way. If you appeared to go with the Mac Tire willingly, I'd have been killed before nightfall."

"Father—"

"They speak of nothing at court but the Seers," Uilleam said, addressing Cailean. Knox's eyes widened, shocked at the dismissal. He was even more shocked at the conversation happening right in front of him. Cailean was a beast, the last prince. How was it Knox's father was so familiar with him? Cailean surely wasn't much older than Knox. How was it Uilleam had known him as a teenager?

"It can no longer be kept secret," Uilleam went on. "There was a time when the Council could charm the court, hold these visions as idle gossip and nonsense. But the Seers persist in their warnings, and now they're spreading."

"Spreading how?" Cailean asked. It rankled that, in this moment, this stranger understood Knox's father better than Knox himself.

"It's beginning to reach the settlements."

Cailean sucked in a ragged breath. "They speak of it as fancy?"

"They speak of it as truth. When it was those drunks hanging around outside the gates, demanding an audience with the Council to tell of the warnings they'd Seen, well. That was plenty easy enough for them to ignore, wasn't it? But now it's the Council's Seers too, and they can't very well turn them out for Seeing things, can they? Not when that's what they get paid for."

Cailean pushed himself to his feet. He walked over to the fire and stood for a long moment with his hands braced on the mantle, his head hung low between his shoulders. Knox was overcome with the nearly irrepressible urge to go and place his hand in the small of Cailean's back, to offer him comfort somehow. He looked away instead, shoving the feeling down.

"Then it's time."

From the doorway, Rhys sucked in a breath. "Brother...."

Cailean spun around, glaring at his sister. "Don't argue with me."

"I've no wish to argue with you. I'm just—it all seems to be happening so quickly."

"Quickly? Rhys, we've been waiting decades. Nothing about this is quick."

"That's not what I mean, Cailean. You know that. But not a month ago—"

"Nothing is as it was a month ago, Rhys."

They said nothing. For a long moment, she and Cailean stared at one another, and it seemed a million unsaid things passed between them. At length, Rhys bowed her head and tilted it, baring her throat to Cailean.

Magic burned hot in Knox's belly, overwhelming him. He tugged the collar of his shirt away from his throat.

"I'm worried," Uilleam said finally, cutting through the awkward tension that lingered. "About our numbers."

Cailean turned to him. "How many are you?"

"It's impossible to know an exact count, but I think a fair estimate is three hundred."

Cailean frowned, his eyebrows knitting together. "That's not what I'd hoped for."

"Nor I. But they are sworn to you."

"Weapons?"

Uilleam shook his head. "Not enough."

"If we were to wait...."

"No," Uilleam cut in. "I think all who can be reached, have been. Time will only weaken their resolve. The Council will find a way to silence the Seers. If there is a time to strike, this is it."

"Strike," Knox said, unable to hold his tongue any longer. "What do you mean, strike? Because it sounds as if you're talking about attacking the Council." He laughed. "You can't be talking about war on the Council. Father, that's treason."

Rhys hissed in a breath. "It would only be treason if the Council had a right to the Phela throne. They do not."

"Even so." Knox shook his head, still not entirely sure what was happening or what part he and his father were playing in it.

"No," Cailean cut in. "This is not up for discussion. If you're not with us—"

"Cailean," Rhys said sharply.

"They have the entire city!" Knox said. "There are thousands of them. And that's assuming you could even cross the ráth to get to them."

"There are Magi in our number," Cailean said. Knox wheeled around on him.

"Not enough. There can't be enough."

"Yet you planned to take on the ráth alone."

"One man can slip through a crack in a wall. But you're talking about taking dozens of men across a magical field. Hundreds of them!"

"And you've drawn us a map of exactly how to get them into the city."

Knox stood, scrubbed his hands over his cheeks. His face was rough, in desperate need of a shave. "This is madness," he muttered. Then something that had been pricking at him for days flared to life in his head; he spun around and pointed a shaking hand at Cailean. "In Dunmore. That barkeep. He called you Mac Tire. But not Jarlath."

"Yes," Cailean said.

"He's human."

"Yes."

"And that's why Yaara panicked. Because she thought he would be killed for being seen with you. For being seen with a Mac Tire."

Cailean held his gaze. Slowly, he nodded once. "Yes."

Rage boiled up in Knox's veins. "And that's why my father was taken. Not because of me. Because of you."

"Knox," Uilleam said, grabbing for his son's arm. "I made this decision ages ago. Decades. I have always been loyal to the Mac Tire. I've been part of the Resistance since you were a babe."

"And you never told me."

"I was trying to keep you safe!"

"And a bloody good job you've done of it! I thought they'd kill you. You'd be dead, and it would be my fault."

"Knox, please," Uilleam said. "I just wanted to protect you. I promised your mother—"

Knox jerked back as though he'd been slapped. "My mother. What in the four seas has my mother got to do with this?"

Silence fell thick on them like a blanket of snow. "Knox," Uilleam said imploringly. The lines on his face cut at Knox's heart. "Please."

"We will send envoys at once," Cailean said. "We must begin preparations."

"War," Knox spat out. "That's what you speak of. When you know the Council will begin snatching boys from their mothers' breasts and arming them with blades too heavy for their young hands. They'll be slaughtered for nothing more than their own ignorance."

"Men have died for less."

"Have you killed for less?"

Cailean didn't answer. He turned to Rhys. "We'll begin tomorrow."

"There will be no peace," Knox said, heart pounding. "If you wage war on the Council, you will slaughter a people who have done nothing to you."

"Peace?" Cailean roared. "Are you mad? Do you imagine for a moment that peace is what I seek? Those men put my father on his knees and made him plead for his wife's life as they took her head— and then they took his. I had four brothers once, and now Rhys and I are all that remain. The last of the great and mighty Phelas." He laughed bitterly. "*Mac Tire*, they call us. Sons of the countryside. And now look at us, driven to this frozen hellscape. This wasteland of misery and death, when the entirety of Ailis belongs to us. There will be no peace in that land until it is under our rule."

"There are good men in those villages, Cailean. There are good men in that city."

"Yes." Cailean nodded. "I'm sure there are. My father was a good man. So were my brothers. So were many of my brethren I've burned, because the ground was too cold to take their bodies. Have you any idea how hard it is to burn a body with frozen wood?"

"Cailean."

"My father was a good man, Knox. I am not. I haven't had that luxury."

SEVEN

IT WAS Rhys who greeted Knox the next day when he stepped out into the brisk morning air. She was perched on a low stone wall that ran straight up the hillside and tumbled into the ruins of the Old city. The hood of her jacket was pulled up over her head, and her long curls spilled out of it and down over her shoulder.

"Good morning," she said, offering Knox the mug curled in her hands. Knox took it and, realizing it was the same thick bitter liquid from his first day there, made a soft "ah" sound and drank deeply from it.

Rhys laughed. "Coffee," she said.

"Sorry?"

"That's coffee. It's good, isn't it?"

"Very. I thought it might be some sort of tea."

Rhys took the mug back from him with a sideways glance. "You've had it before?"

"The first morning I was here," Knox said. He sat down on the wall beside her, hissing as the cold of the stone crept through his thin pants. "Well, afternoon, I suppose."

"Cailean made you coffee?"

"I...." Knox pulled his legs up and looked out over the horizon. This far north, the sky was so clear, he felt he could see forever. "I suppose?"

"Cailean doesn't drink coffee."

"All right," Knox said slowly, trying to puzzle out why Rhys was telling him this. It was too early to think of Cailean. Knox had been up for all hours, tossing and turning in front of the fire, thinking about Cailean. To his side, Uilleam had slept soundly, his face turned into the quilts Rhys had provided them to make a pallet in the sitting room. Knox had stared at his father's face for ages, grateful to have him back but overwhelmed by the news he brought with him.

Rhys sighed. "He's not all bad, you know."

Knox laughed dryly. "You're his sister."

"This has been his burden since he was hardly a year old. He never asked for this."

"It's been my experience that men never ask for this sort of thing," Knox said. "A man's lot isn't his measure."

"You disapprove of his plans."

"How could I not? People are going to die if he goes through with this."

"Better they should live imprisoned by the Council? Knox, the magic in this land that sustains us, it is seeping away. The land is angry, and until the Mac Tire return to power—"

Knox groaned and tipped his head back. "Rhys. It's so early. Must we start the morning like this?"

To his side, Rhys laughed softly, her shoulders shaking. "I've been up for hours. You humans. I forget."

"Yes," Knox said, temper rising. "Us humans. So feeble and useless."

"Wait, Knox, please." Rhys reached out for him. "I didn't mean it like that, come on. Please?" She offered him the coffee and a small smile. "Coffee?"

Knox shook his head and accepted the cup. He took a deep sip; the drink warmed him down to his toes. "I don't know how we're supposed to make this work."

"Time will reveal the way," Rhys said confidently. "I'm sure of it."

"Time's the thing we don't have."

Rhys laughed again. "How old are you?"

"Twenty."

"Believe me when I tell you that this is nothing to do with you being a human, only with you being so young. Trust me, we've time enough."

"So young? You can't have five years on me."

"Five? Bless you, Knox, it's more like fifteen."

"Fifteen? So you're older than Cailean?"

"I've nearly ten years on him," Rhys replied. "He's the baby of the family. I was right in the middle. Two brothers before me, three after. I was my parents' only daughter."

"But… if you're so much older than Cailean, why is he the heir and not you? Do Mac Tire not recognize women as leaders?"

A glance over revealed a smile curving across Rhys's pretty face. "Oh, no, we do. But Lia Fáil did not cry out for me."

"Lia Fáil?" Did the beasts ever speak in a way that made sense? "I don't know what you mean."

"No," Rhys said. "I expect you don't. I was never meant for the throne. Lia Fáil chose my brother, George." Rhys turned to him. "He was killed on his twelfth birthday."

"Oh." Knox hardly knew what to say. "I'm sorry."

For long moments, they sat in silence, passing the mug back and forth between them. When it was empty, Rhys stood and brushed the dirt from her pants.

"What about Cailean?" Knox said, tipping his face to peer up at her. "Did Lia Fáil cry out for him?"

"No," Rhys said. She glanced out over the frostbitten trees before them. "No, but she will."

She made her way inside, leaving Knox to himself. He thought to follow her, but the coffee had warmed him through, and it was nice to sit in the quiet for a while and watch the world come to life. Knox let his magic fill him up, seeping through his skin. There were countless little rodents and birds scurrying about and fluttering here and there, gathering up worms and crickets. Most of the smaller animals would still be bedded down in this cold, but there were a few moose and a handful of deer scattered a mile or two to the east. Knox closed his eyes and soaked up the warmth of their life.

"What are you thinking about?"

Knox looked up and found his father standing above him. Knox shielded his eyes from the sun. "Egan," he said. "I hope she's all right."

Uilleam made a soft noise and sat down beside Knox. "They'll have taken her back to the city."

"And sold her," Knox said. His heart hurt at the very idea.

"Have you ever wondered why I do not speak of your mother's family?"

Knox swiveled around. He'd longed to know more about his mother but had always assumed the subject was too painful for his father to speak of. Knocked askance by the abrupt change of subject, Knox could do no more than shake his head before his father went on.

"They are an old family, going back ages. Your great-great grandmother was a baker in the castle when Cailean's great-great grandmother ruled. You know how people are, Knox. Their memories are long."

"All right?" Knox said uncertainly. "I don't understand."

"Your mother was sympathetic to the Resistance before it ever really existed. When the Council took the city, Shae was devastated. She felt the entire revolt an injustice, and she let everyone know about it. And the Council, for however vile they are now, it's nothing like the bloodlust that ruled them then. There was no room for dissent."

A sick feeling of dread turned Knox's stomach. He swallowed the bile that ripped his throat. "Father, what are you saying?"

Uilleam stared out over the land, his shoulders hunched.

"They… they killed her," Knox forced out, because sure as the sun was rising in the east, Uilleam could not bring himself to give voice to the words.

Tears crowded Uilleam's eyes. He nodded sharply. "Shortly after her death, testimony was given to the Council that she'd been part of the Resistance. No testimony was given against me, so there was little they could do, but you were already showing signs of magic. It was too big of a risk to have their gaze upon us." He looked away, wiping at the corner of his eye. "I formally severed relations with Shea's family before your third year. I have not seen them since."

"Formally?" Knox whispered. "What does that mean?"

"It means we are no longer family. That I reject your mother as my wife."

"But—" Tears burned hot at the back of Knox's eyes. He could not seem to clear the hard lump in his throat. "But why? You loved her. I know you did."

"Of course I did, Knox. I loved her like… like my own body. I miss her every day. Oh, God, and you look so like her sometimes, I can hardly stand it. But she was gone, and we wanted to protect you. It was the only way we could be sure."

"We?"

"Her parents and I. There were no charges leveled against them either, but it wasn't a risk any of us could take. They fled. I don't know where they are now."

"So I have grandparents?"

Uilleam nodded and offered a weak smile. "And an uncle. She had a brother."

"You never told me."

"How could I?" Uilleam asked. "There were too many questions you'd ask that I couldn't answer."

"You never told me my mother was murdered. You never told me. How could I not have known that? How could I *not have known*?"

Rage that shocked Knox with its intensity surged through him, and he was on his feet without meaning to, was half a mile into the woods without realizing it. Red blurred the edges of his vision as he ran, snapping twigs and crunching through leaves, dazed with the fury that burned up the empty space in his chest. He ran until his lungs heaved with it, his breath fogged in front of him, and Knox pushed through it all. He ran until he thought his heart would explode.

Then he stopped and bent down, bracing himself with hands to his knees.

His mother had been killed—been murdered. She hadn't died of a fever, the way Uilleam had said. Knox's every thought of her was false. She had been murdered, and Knox's mind raced through horrible pictures, flipping through them rapidly, one after the other: his mother with her throat slit, her blood crimson on the dirt; his mother hung as a traitor; his mother put down like a rabid dog, daggers tearing open her flesh.

He had never known. How had he never known?

The scream that tore from Knox's throat was raw and primal. His magic burst from him with such force he thought it would rip a hole in his very soul.

An army of birds took to the sky, screeching their terror as their homes jerked and shook. The trees, some as thick around as a man's thigh, swayed like newborn blades of grass. The boulders that rose up in front of him trembled; then, with a mighty sound, they exploded into shards that were carried toward him on a wind of Knox's magic. They did not cut his clothes or pierce his skin, but instead skated right around him, like water around stones in a river.

The wind howled bitterly as Knox sank to his knees on the forest floor, but he did not feel the cold. This truth, kept from him so long, made a fire of his heart, and not even the desperate cold of the mountains could touch it.

How foolish he had been. How childish. He had believed himself so important, the only person capable of saving his father. And the whole time, it had been his father saving him. A whole great world churning and changing right before Knox's eyes, and he hadn't even realized it.

There was no question now what he must do. The Council had killed his mother. They had killed Cailean's entire family. Given the chance, they would kill the rest of them. There was no choice but to end it.

Kneeling there in the dirt and rocks and dust, Knox remembered something his mother had whispered to him when he was no more than a toddler.

The wolves were of magic, she'd said, and magic loved them.

Knox looked up. He filled his lungs with the clean scent of winter: the evergreens, the leaves that had been churned to mulch by passing wildlife, the earth he'd overturned in his furor. Then he held out his hands and created a small fire that he could cup in his palms. The flames were beautiful, a thousand hues of red and orange and gold. They did not burn Knox, but he knew if he placed them upon the ground and wished it, a wind would carry their sparks up and up and up until the tallest of the pine trees burned.

The walk back to the house was quiet. Knox's feet carried him forward with purpose. Cailean was waiting outside for him, his arms crossed over his broad chest.

Knox stepped up to him and tipped his head back to look him fully in the eyes. They seemed to contain as many shades as Knox's fire had.

"You asked me about loyalty."

"Yes," Cailean said.

"You have mine."

Cailean sucked in a sharp breath but did not look away. He looked at Knox for a long moment, then nodded firmly.

"Your magic."

"It's for you," Knox said simply, and then, wondering if that was too clear, corrected himself. "Unto the service of the Mac Tire. I think I've known it since I first saw you. It… recognizes you. This land recognizes you."

"The Council will brand you a traitor. You'll be hung on sight."

"Yes," Knox said, nodding. "Same as my mother."

"She was highly spoken of," Cailean said, and Knox tried not to feel a sadness that Cailean knew more of his mother's truth than he did. "She was well missed."

"She *is* well missed."

Cailean's gaze softened. "Yes," he said. "She is."

"Will you—will you take my faithfulness?" Knox asked, suddenly unsure. He was willing to swear an oath to Cailean now, eager perhaps, because it was quite clear to him that the Mac Tire weren't the beasts. It was the Council who ruled like animals.

"You've already given it," Cailean said, but he lifted a hand and placed it carefully on the crown of Knox's head. "Unto the service of the rightful heir of Ailis, do you commend your magic?"

"I do."

Cailean's hand was warm and heavy. Knox had the mad thought that he'd like to feel that immovable weight on him at length, steadying him. But as soon as the thought had slipped into his mind, Cailean was moving away, his feet scuffing over the stones. He disappeared into the house, and the door snapped shut behind him.

Knox lifted his head and stared at the space where he had been.

By the time Knox felt himself calm enough to enter the house, Rhys, Uilleam, and Cailean were seated around the table with their heads bent together. Rhys acknowledged Knox with a quick wave of her hand; Uilleam looked up, worry etched on his face, and gave Knox a questioning smile.

Knox responded in kind. He was still upset with his father, was still hurt at being lied to, but understood Uilleam had simply been doing all a father could be expected to do: trying to keep his son safe.

Cailean, though, did not even glance up. His head was bent low over the papers on the table, Knox's map among them.

"Yaara and Anne await you, and together you'll travel to Greenfall," Cailean was saying. "Uilleam, who do you have there?"

"Herik, the butcher."

"And you'll be well met?"

"Certainly," Uilleam replied. "A great number are with us. Aside from Darry, it is our strongest held settlement."

"Darry?" Knox asked, surprised. "We have men in Darry?"

At this Cailean did look up, but if he was surprised to hear Knox including himself in the plans, he did not show it. In fact his face showed nothing as he said: "Your father has built up a lifetime's worth of connections there. Darry is the heart of the Resistance."

Knox shook his head. "I had no idea."

Cailean considered him for a moment, then returned to his papers. "Knox and I will travel north into Cairn. We'll join their forces and meet you in Whit."

"Why don't I travel with my father?"

"You're not safe together," Cailean said. "As sure as we are plotting, so too is the Council. Your faces are known to them. If they see either of you...." He trailed off, but Knox knew what he was leaving unsaid. He and Uilleam would be killed without a second thought. And while Knox might be able to use his magic to protect himself, Uilleam was vulnerable.

"All right, then," Knox said. "That's that, isn't it?"

"It is," Cailean said, effectively ending the discussion.

"All right," Knox repeated.

Preparing for Uilleam to leave was a simple task. He had arrived with nothing more than the clothes on his back and was leaving with little more. He and Cailean were of a similar size, so Uilleam swapped his threadbare pants for some that were in better repair and accepted an old pack stuffed with spiced meat, coarse bread, and a few dented metal jars to hold water. Knox sat on the floor and watched him carefully arrange his things away, trying all the while not to think of what had happened to their belongings at their small home in Darry.

Rhys's departure was to be a more complicated affair. She had lived in the tiny house for six years, and while she swore she was not sorry to leave it, she still had half a decade's belongings tucked away there.

"None of it is important," she said finally, abandoning her attempts to sort through the books on the low shelf that separated the kitchen from the sitting room. She sat on the floor in the middle of piles of books, one large volume in each hand. She dropped them both to the ground and stood up, dusting her hands off and kicking the books toward the shelf. "Besides, I can come back for it once we're reinstated in Forradh."

"Forradh?" Knox asked.

"Cahircluain to you," Rhys explained. "Fortress in the field." A sour look crossed her face. "Forradh to us. The royal seat."

They divided the pots and pans between them, lashing them to Uilleam and Rhys's packs, putting aside some of them for Knox and Cailean to carry with them, and leaving the largest and heaviest to be scavenged or eaten up by the passage of time.

Uilleam and Rhys left the next day, bellies full and hoods pulled up against the cold. Having been reunited with his father so recently, Knox was not at all keen to bid him farewell again, but he forced himself to focus on the fire in his chest as he embraced Uilleam, pressing into the cushion of his father's coat.

"Be safe," he bade him.

"And you," Uilleam said. He pushed him out to arm's length and stared into Knox's eyes. "Listen to Cailean. Trust only him. And don't be foolish."

Cailean walked over to them, heedless of the good-bye he was interrupting. Knox would have protested, but then Cailean did something that stopped him in his tracks. He stepped into Uilleam's space and lifted a hand to touch Uilleam's neck.

Uilleam's eyes went wide and silent as Cailean tugged him forward and brushed his cheek over Uilleam's. It was done in a perfunctory way, not with the affection Cailean had shown Rhys, or even Yaara or Anne, but it was made clear by Uilleam's shocked face when Cailean pulled away that something of importance had passed between them.

"I give you leave," Cailean said, letting go of Uilleam's neck. "And I pray you safe travel."

Uilleam nodded and staggered backward.

For a moment everything around them stood still: the woods, the land, even the sky seemed to pause for them. The moment stretched on and on, until it was almost painful to stand in. Then a raven crowed overhead, and Rhys stepped forward and pressed her cheek to Cailean's.

Cailean exhaled and leaned into her. He seemed to sag into her body, letting her take his weight. Her arms went round his waist. She had to press up onto her toes to lean her head on his shoulder. Cailean murmured something into her ear, and she nodded. Knox could not hear him, but then again, he certainly was not meant to.

"Brother," Rhys replied. She touched her hand to Cailean's chest, over his heart, and Knox found he had to look away from the naked affection between them. The transparency in the way they were with one another made Knox shift uncomfortably. He glanced over and found Uilleam looking at him with wet eyes. For all their differences, maybe family was always the same.

"I'll see you soon," Uilleam said. He stepped forward and embraced Knox again. Knox clung to him. "Take care, I beg you."

Knox squeezed him so tightly he thought Uilleam might not be able to breathe. "And you," he said. "Please, take the utmost care."

A soft voice pried them apart. "We need to go," Rhys said, laying her hand on Uilleam's back.

They shouldered their packs and took their leave, crunching through the grass as they set out for the tree line. It was foolish to stand in the cold and watch them, but Knox and Cailean stood, shoulder to shoulder, and looked out into the forest long past the point when Rhys and Uilleam had been swallowed up by the trees.

Then, as one, they turned and went inside.

EIGHT

"CARDS," KNOX said, motioning at the bookcase. "Dice? Nothing at all?"

Cailean shook his head, his face as impassive as ever as he watched Knox ping around the house like a caged cat. Knox yanked his sleeves down over his hands, sick with nerves. Two hours. His father had been gone two hours. If he left now, right now, and ran as fast as he could, or if he could summon a horse from somewhere…. Perhaps there were some wild mares in the valley, and if Knox headed that way before the sun set and the cold set in, if he could find a suitable horse within the hour, he could move much faster than Uilleam, and….

"Knox," Cailean said sharply. "You look like you're going to have a fit. Calm down."

"Calm down?" Knox said. Even to his own ears, his voice was strangely hysterical. "Calm down? It'll be a bloody miracle if I see my father alive again, and you're telling me to calm down?"

"Your optimism is overwhelming."

"Optimism? We're about to march on a fortress surrounded by the greatest Magi in the kingdom and—"

"Not the greatest," Cailean said.

Knox blew out a frustrated breath. "I'm one man, Cailean."

"And you've a powerful magic, Knox."

The chair creaked under Knox's weight as he folded himself down into it. He propped his elbows on his knees and dropped his head into his hands. "I shouldn't have let him go without me."

"Rhys will look after him," Cailean said. His voice was soft and close. Knox lifted his head and found Cailean kneeling down in front of him, head tilted to one side. "She will. On her life, she'll take care of him."

Knox's heart lurched selfishly. It was unfair how comforting that was to hear, when Rhys was all the family Cailean could claim for himself, just as Uilleam was it for Knox.

"She's your sister."

"He's your father."

This close, Cailean's eyes looked like exploding stars—a thousand points of tiny blue light that Knox found he couldn't look away from. Without really intending to—without even realizing he was doing it until it was already happening—Knox lifted his hand and touched the sharp edge of Cailean's cheekbone.

Beneath his hand, a muscle twitched. Cailean's jaw clenched as Knox flattened his palm, still staring into Cailean's eyes. Then Cailean's eyes slid shut and Knox slid his hand lower, fingertips dragging over the stubbled skin of Cailean's cheek. His skin frizzled, his magic like sparks off a flint as it curled tightly in on itself in his belly, seemingly ready to flare out toward the warmth of Cailean's body.

Cailean's breath grew labored as Knox's hand wandered farther down, over the curve of Cailean's mouth, the dip just beneath it. His chin was a sharp point that led down to the long, soft column of—

Knox jerked as Cailean's hand shot out, his eyes flying open, his fingers wrapping tightly around Knox's wrist.

"I—" Knox began, cheeks heating as he tried to fumble out an apology, but Cailean just shook his head.

"Not—not there." The room was silent as Cailean lifted Knox's hand and then moved it down slowly. Knox watched, his heart thumping wildly, teetering on the edge of complete abandon as Cailean uncurled Knox's fingers and pressed them to his chest. "Here."

The muscles of Cailean's chest were firm under Knox's touch, and beneath that, his heart beat out a steady rhythm Knox could feel against his palm.

"What are we doing?" he whispered, glancing up to find Cailean's eyes still shut. Cailean didn't answer right away, and it was... nice, almost, having a moment to look at Cailean without worrying about being caught. He was so beautiful. His hair was so dark and his skin so smooth. It seemed odd, somehow, that someone so strong, so mighty and terrifying, could be this still. This soft.

"Distracting ourselves," Cailean said at length.

"Yeah?"

"Yes," Cailean said, and he pushed into Knox's space and pressed their mouths together.

Knox's body responded before he'd made the decision. His fingers clenched, burying themselves in the fabric of Cailean's shirt, and he shoved forward into the kiss. He was clumsy, but it didn't matter, because Cailean was clutching his hips and hauling him to the edge of the chair so that Knox was perched precariously, most of his weight balanced on Cailean.

Cailean kissed the same way he did everything else: with a quiet intensity that was unnerving if Knox thought about it too long. His hands were hot on Knox's skin, spread wide and claiming, and his mouth was intoxicating. Knox drank from it, brave beyond his own experience, sliding his tongue into Cailean's mouth.

"Is this—" Cailean gasped out, pressing his forehead to Knox's only to angle his head the other way and capture him in another kiss. A groan slipped out of Knox's mouth and into Cailean's.

"Is it what?"

"Is this all right?" Cailean asked.

Knox couldn't let himself think. His mind was already trying to run away from him. Instead of answering, he slid out of the chair and onto Cailean's lap, and Cailean took him easily, skimming his big hands around Knox's hips and under the edge of his shirt.

The floor was cold beneath them, but Knox paid it no mind. He'd had a fumble or two back home in Darry, but they were all just good fun, nothing like this—never anything that made him feel like his body would give up if he stopped even for a moment. "Kiss me," he demanded, and Cailean twisted under Knox, wrapping one arm tightly around his waist and planting the other on the floor so he could lift up and roll Knox beneath him.

And still they kissed, their mouths slotting together again and again until Knox thought he would go mad from it. He arched up into Cailean's chest, wanting the weight of it on him. Cailean obliged. He nudged Knox's thighs apart and settled into the cradle of them, then propped himself up with one forearm framing either side of Knox's head.

He opened his mouth as if to speak, but Knox didn't want words. He didn't want to talk or even think. He wrapped his arms around Cailean's neck and yanked him down so that their bodies crashed together. Knox's prick was already hard in his pants, and when Cailean rolled his hips against it, Knox tightened his arms and groaned.

"Like this," Cailean muttered into Knox's mouth, shoving his hips down again and again, forcing Knox to hang on and ride the movement of it. "Like this, yeah?"

Knox would have liked to get his clothes off—to get Cailean's clothes off for that matter—and feel those miles of warm skin against his own. But the pain of their movement, the ache each time Cailean ground into him, gave Knox enough of a distraction from the pleasure building in his body that he didn't go off like an exploding star as soon as Cailean brought their mouths together.

The air in the room was cold, but he barely noticed. He wrapped one leg around Cailean's hips, pressed his foot into the back of Cailean's thigh, and shoved up against him, hardly able to breathe around how *good* it was.

"You're so—" Cailean bit out, dropping his chin to his chest and panting down at Knox. "So—tides, Knox."

Deeper and deeper into his pleasure Knox sank, until he thought he would happily lie on this floor for the rest of his life and let Cailean move above him and against him. But long before he wished it, he felt the tiny spark of pleasure in his stomach begin, and though he wanted this to go on and on and never end, he was helpless to do anything except grab onto that pleasure as it coiled tighter and tighter, burning so bright around the edges.

"Close," he managed. He dug his fingers into Cailean's shoulders and squeezed his eyes shut.

His orgasm punched out of him with such force that Knox lost his breath. It crested and ebbed, then welled up again. Knox clung to Cailean and clung to his pleasure, breathless and dazed, until above him, Cailean shouted, jerked forward one last time, then sagged against him, his face red and sweaty and beautiful, beautiful, beautiful.

THE SUN was little more than a sliver of pink light behind the mountains when they rose in the morning. Knox lingered in bed for a moment, watching the play of muscles in Cailean's back as he drew on his clothes. He was reluctant to leave the warmth of the bed, not knowing when such a comfort would present itself to him again, but the sooner he rose, the sooner they set off, the sooner Knox would see his father again. And it was with that thought that he pushed the quilts aside and stood. He shivered as his bare feet landed on the floor.

Cailean turned and threw him a glance over his shoulder. He paused, a look on his face that made it clear he wished to say something. Then he gave a tiny shake of his head and dragged another sweater over his shoulders. "I'll make coffee."

Knox wrapped his arms around himself. If Cailean wasn't going to say anything about last night, neither was he. It wouldn't do to talk about it. Indeed, there was nothing to talk about. It had been a distraction—a welcome one, but a distraction nonetheless. "I thought you didn't drink coffee?"

Cailean shrugged. "I'll drink anything if it's warm enough."

Then he turned and left, closing the door behind him.

It took a matter of minutes for Knox to pack his things. All of his belongings fit easily into his old pack, leaving plenty of room for the heavy cloaks and sweaters Cailean had pulled out for him. Knox tucked his map, carefully folded, into his wooden box of bullets, then wrapped the box in an extra blanket.

"Breakfast," Cailean said, when Knox had made his way downstairs. They ate a quiet meal of cold potatoes and coffee. Knox tried not to smile at the way Cailean winced with every sip he took of the bitter liquid.

"Why do you drink it if you hate it?"

Cailean drained his cup. He stood up and looked around the room. Knox stuffed the last of his potatoes into his cheek and followed Cailean's gaze around the house. The grate stood empty, and the wood burning stove sat cold and black. Rhys had taken very few of her belongings with her, but the rooms seemed hollow without her in them.

"Ready?"

"Is that all?" Knox asked, gesturing around the room.

"Rhys will come back for her things once… once it's over."

The cold was biting so early in the morning. It grabbed at Knox's nose and fingertips, making him shout and shove his hands into his armpits.

"Hell!"

Cailean gave him a grim smile. "It'll get no better. Are you warm enough?"

"If I had on one more sweater I wouldn't be able to move."

"On that note," Cailean said. "You know we're going north? Into the mountains?"

"Just the foot of them?" Knox said quickly, because cloaks and sweaters or not, he was ill equipped for a mountain passage.

"Just the foot of them," Cailean assured him. "But the farther north we get, this terrain will be…." He shook his head. "At times, I may have to carry you."

Knox raised his eyebrows, hardly able to contain how little of a chance there was of that ever happening. But the thin line of Cailean's mouth made him hold his tongue.

"Right," he said. "Then I guess we've no time to spare, have we?"

He looped his arms through his pack and followed Cailean toward the tree line. Neither of them looked back.

THE BLOW came when Knox was least expecting it. One moment he was gathering up rocks for a fire ring; the next he was on his back blinking up at Cailean.

"Tides!" Knox shouted. "What the blazes did you do that for?"

"You've got elemental magic, Knox. Bloody use it."

Knox sat up and rubbed the back of his head, glaring furiously at Cailean. "You punched me in the back of the head because I didn't start a fire the way you wanted?"

"No," Cailean said slowly, like Knox was an idiot. Hell, maybe he was. Maybe tromping off in the woods with a wolf he barely knew and then turning his back on him was a completely idiotic move. "You're never aware of your surroundings. I could have been anyone. You'd have been dead before you hit the ground."

"So that was what? A life lesson?"

Cailean shrugged. "Survival, Knox. If you want to survive, keep your wits about you. Don't turn your back on anyone."

"You're not anyone," Knox burst out. "I assumed you *had* my back. Partners, yeah?"

The temperature had been dropping steadily as they moved north. Exhausted, hungry, and frozen through to his spine by the brutal wind, Knox had no desire for Cailean's lessons, useful though they might have been. The blow hadn't had Cailean's weight behind it, certainly, but Knox's skin was hypersensitive from the cold, and every bit of it that was exposed to the air stung. A punch in the head was the very last thing he was in the mood for.

"I'll start supper," Cailean said, holding out a hand. Knox glared at it but allowed Cailean to pull him to his feet.

"I'll finish the damn fire." He turned back to the overgrown cement walls where he and Cailean had stopped to make shelter. Whatever this building had been once, most of it was gone now, but two walls remained and provided some measure of protection against the wind that howled through the trees.

"Look—"

"I know," Knox shouted. "Watch my back, got it."

"No," Cailean said. He motioned to the corner. "Look."

Knox looked over and found a fire already roaring in the flat place he'd created for it.

"If you can learn to control that...." Cailean said. He left the rest unsaid and turned to his pack. For a brief moment, Knox considered going over and whacking *him* on the head, but in the end his curiosity won out. He stepped up to the fire and watched it jump and leap.

"Can you move rocks?"

"What?"

"Rocks," Cailean said. He motioned to where he had piled fist-sized rocks by the shelter wall. "Can you move them?"

"You can't move those rocks?" Knox asked. "I thought you were supposed to be so powerful and—"

Cailean shut him up by walking over, reaching past Knox, and pushing over a boulder that had knocked a hole clean through the wall.

"Oh."

"I'm asking if you can move *those* rocks."

"Is this some sort of test? Like the punching thing? Because I have to tell you—"

"Knox!" Cailean roared. "Can you or can you not magic those blasted rocks into the fire?"

"I have no idea!"

Toe-to-toe, they stared at one another, faces inches apart. They were breathing so hard Knox could feel the heat of it on his frozen cheeks.

Knox couldn't decide if he wanted to hit Cailean or kiss him.

"Then try."

With no idea of how to even begin, Knox turned to the pile of stones. He glanced at them, then at Cailean, then at the fire. "I don't...."

"Just try," Cailean said. Knox looked down to see Cailean's fingers closing around his wrist. When he looked up, the rocks were shimmering, trembling where they sat. The next moment, they zoomed through the air and deposited themselves in the fire's heart. The flames leapt.

A smile broke over Cailean's face. Knox's entire body thrilled.

"I'll start dinner," Cailean said, and he squeezed Knox's wrist once more before pulling away. He turned and pulled a heavy cast iron pan from his bag.

"You packed that?" Knox asked, raising his brows.

Cailean looked from the pan, to Knox, then back to the pan. "Yes?"

"It has to weigh a ton."

Cailean huffed out a breath, then returned to rummaging around in his bag.

"Right," Knox muttered. "No pan is too heavy for a Mac Tire to haul across the bleeding mountains, even if it weighs a ton." He sat down and began digging his blankets out of his bag. At least the ruin they'd found was enough to shelter them from the wind. A slight overhang was left, and Knox dragged his things underneath it, in case snow came that night. It was certainly cold enough.

The sweet smell of milled corn pulled Knox's attention back to the fire.

"What's that?" he asked, coming over to peer at Cailean's skillet. "Is that cornbread?"

"Still want to make fun of the pan?"

"Not even a little," Knox replied, miming locking his lips.

After they ate, Cailean dragged things to the overhang where Knox had left his bag. "Here?" he asked.

To sleep. He clearly meant here to sleep. Knox tried not to read anything into that. Just because they'd tumbled the night before…. It didn't mean anything. Not really.

"Um," Knox said. The weather being what it was, having a warm body close to him all night sounded heavenly. "I thought under there, in case it snows?"

"Right." Cailean grabbed his blankets and tossed them into a pile with Knox's. "Move those for me, will you?"

"Move them?" Knox gestured around. "Move them where?"

"Just away. A few feet. I don't want to get more dirt on them than I have to."

Confused, but too full and sated from the warmth of dinner, Knox did as Cailean bade him. He picked up the blankets and moved the lot of them to the other side of their camp. When he turned back around, Cailean had his claws extended and was on his knees, clawing at the dirt.

"What are you doing?" Knox asked, heartbeat going quick at the sight of those claws.

"Do you want to freeze tonight?"

"Not particularly, no."

"Nor I," Cailean said. He turned back to his work, and as Knox watched, Cailean dug a deep trench under the overhang that was at least six feet long.

"Now," he said. "The rocks."

"The *rocks*?"

"The ones you put in the fire. Bring them over here."

It was the work of a thought. The rocks, white hot and crackling, lifted up on an invisible cloud of magic. Cailean stepped back as Knox directed them into the trench. "Like this?"

"Just like that," Cailean answered with a grin. When the trench was filled, Cailean bent to cover them with dirt, but Knox shook his head.

"Let me try," he said.

Cailean nodded and watched with a smile playing on his lips as Knox lifted the dirt and dropped it down over top of the rocks.

"Good?"

"Good," Cailean replied. "Give it half an hour for the water to bake out of the dirt, and then we can put our bed down."

Our bed. Knox tried not to shiver and, failing miserably, hoped it passed as the chill.

Knox sat near the remains of the fire as he waited. He let his magic loose, sending out little tendrils of it to the nearby animals. There weren't many—a few foxes and a wild boar—but it warmed Knox to feel their energy tangle with his, even if only for a moment.

"It should be fine now," Cailean said at length. He hauled their blankets back to the spot where Knox had laid the stones and spread them out. Knox hurried into them, because the fire was dying and the cold was seeping into his bones. It was the sort of cold that made his whole body draw up, made his teeth chatter and his shoulders ache.

"Scoot over," Cailean said. He climbed in beside Knox and tugged the blankets up around them. Knox found himself sliding as close as he could to Cailean without touching him. The heat from the rocks buried in the ground was lovely, but not nearly as desirable as the heat that came from Cailean in waves.

Cailean sighed softly and pulled the blankets up over their heads. It felt like a secret, the tiny, quiet space between them. It was too dark to make out anything other than the bright whites of Cailean's eyes.

"Are you tired?" Knox whispered.

The blankets rustled as Cailean shook his head. His hand was warm when it nudged Knox's hip. "You?"

"Exhausted," Knox replied, but he closed the space between them and opened up for Cailean's kiss.

Knox's mind went blank. He could not grasp a single thought that had to do with anything except Cailean—there was his warm breath and there were his fingers carding into Knox's hair. There was the secret sound he made when he was kissing and yes, there was his tongue, deliberately swiping along Knox's bottom lip.

"Cailean," he murmured.

Cailean answered by sliding his hand under Knox's shirt and smoothing it over his stomach. He made a soft, secret sound into Knox's mouth and tugged him close.

Knox lurched into action. He grabbed at Cailean—inelegantly, but with no less meaning than if he'd swept him off his feet—and wound up with one hand on Cailean's hip and one tangled in his hair. Cailean's laughter was a burst of air across Knox's mouth. Knox swallowed the sound and slanted his mouth under Cailean's, unable to close his eyes for fear that this would slip away from him.

Knox's hands trembled in the darkness. He tilted his head one way, then the other, learning how their mouths fit together, discovering a deep well of knowledge in just that touch. He wasn't bold; his hands shook until Cailean groaned and rolled Knox beneath him. His knees came to rest on either side of Knox's hips. Then it was ever so easy to open his mouth and let his tongue slide against Cailean's, and all the while, Cailean made the most delicious sounds that Knox thought he could happily drown in.

Knox moaned a little without meaning to, tightening his grip on Cailean's waist. Cailean made a happy, wanting sound low in his throat, and Knox found himself pulling his mouth free so he could dip his head and press his lips to the curve of Cailean's throat.

"Come back up here," Cailean rasped out, and Knox found his mouth again and let himself be kissed until he went dizzy with it. Eventually he had to pull away to breathe, but he didn't get far. Cailean caught him with a warm palm to the back of his neck, holding him so that their foreheads pressed together and Knox was breathing the air from Cailean's kiss.

Cailean's kisses were slow and drugging. Knox opened his mouth to it, barely able to keep up.

"How do you want me?" Knox finally asked, coloring.

"Like this," Cailean answered. "Just like this." He sat back on his heels, taking the blankets with him. Knox gasped and struggled up onto his elbows, searching for the warmth and getting stuck halfway there when the pale light of the evening came rushing in.

Knox knew his body was thin and pale and nothing to look at. But Cailean… Cailean was a maze of hard muscles and golden skin, and Knox thought that if he were allowed to look forever, he might never get tired of it. He might look forever without ever wanting to do anything else ever again.

"This?" he asked eventually. He ran his hands up Cailean's thighs, traced a knuckle down the length of his hard prick.

"Tides," Cailean gasped, throwing his head back and swearing up at the sky. "Knox. You'll be the death of me."

Knox buried his grin in his shoulders. He knew he was nothing, not compared to Cailean, but still Cailean wanted him, pale and skinny and flawed as he was. There was power in it, and Knox was drunk on it. He wrapped his fist around Cailean's length and began to move his hand, loving the warm weight of Cailean, loving the way he shook and gasped and begged.

"Wait," Cailean gasped out. "Wait, oh tides, wait. Let me touch you."

Knox loosened his grip and stared wildly at Cailean as he slid down the length of his body and rolled them over, nudging him until Knox settled into the cradle of his thighs. His dick slid into the hollow of Knox's hip.

"Oh," Knox said, eyes flying open.

"Like this," Cailean said, reaching down to draw Knox's prick out of his pants, then wrapping his long fingers around both of them. "Like this, yeah?"

Knox forced himself to nod and coaxed his hips forward. His mouth fell open as, shuddering and overwhelmed with sensation, Cailean arched his back, pushing his hips up and rubbing his dick along the underside of Knox's.

"Oh my," Knox said, staring down at Cailean, sprawled across the blankets beneath him. "I can't—you're beautiful."

Pleasure welled up inside him as they moved together, gathering in his body and making his toes curl. He clenched his jaw and tried to hold on, but the sight of Cailean beneath him was too much.

"I'm gonna…" he choked out.

"Wait," Cailean groaned, tightening his grip and quickening his pace. "Just… wait, wait."

He leaned up for another kiss at the same time that Knox reached a hand between their sweaty bodies and tangled his fingers with Cailean's. Cailean gasped and stilled, the muscles in his stomach going taut.

"Now, now," he gasped into Knox's mouth, and Knox found that suddenly, he had no choice in it. He came with a shiver that turned into a quaking as Cailean's cock jerked against his own. His pleasure tore from him and stole his breath, unfurling beneath his skin. Their bellies and hips went slick with come as they worked their hands in tandem.

Eventually, Knox uncurled his wet fingers, and Cailean followed him. Their mouths were still pressed together, and they passed a breath back and forth, suspended together in the silence. Finally Cailean rolled onto his side, wiped his hand on the blanket, and tugged Knox against him. Knox went easily, perfectly contented and, for the first time he could remember, in want of nothing.

NINE

"TELL ME about Lia Fáil."

For the first time since Knox had met him, Cailean stumbled. "How do you know of Lia Fáil?" he asked as he regained his balance.

Then, as one, they said, "Rhys."

"Of course," Cailean said.

For several moments, nothing more passed between them. Cailean did not seem inclined to answer, and Knox was too cold to think of anything else to say. He had been thinking about Rhys's words these past few days as he and Cailean slowly made their way to Cairn, but still could not puzzle out what Rhys had meant when she said that Lia Fáil would cry out for Cailean.

"Please, Cailean," Knox said at length. "I'm frozen to my core. Talk to me. Distract me so I forget I can't feel my feet."

Cailean did not even pause. "Is that hyperbole, or can you truly not feel your feet?"

Knox stamped his feet. "Oh, I can feel them, all right. Feels like I'm being eaten alive by ants. Is that good or bad?"

"Bad, probably."

"I thought as much."

"Lia Fáil is a stone," Cailean said. "Was a stone. It's probably gone now."

"But what was it?"

Cailean heaved a great sigh. "To you, the place is a city, nothing more. But to us—"

"Forradh," Knox supplied. "The royal seat."

Cailean nodded. "And in the great courtyard, there is a ring of stones. In the center stands Lia Fáil, taller than any man. Taller than any Mac Tire. And she chooses our ruler."

"How?"

"She cries out for us," Cailean said simply, picking his way through a thicket of brambles and thorns. "Children are brought forth to her, and she chooses the rightful heir."

"Any children?" Knox asked. "Or only the children of the king?"

"Anyone may come," Cailean said. "The stone is in a courtyard open to the whole of the kingdom. Though if Lia Fáil cried out for someone else...."

"What would happen?"

Cailean's eyes were hard when they met Knox's. "I have no idea. She never has."

The frozen ground crunched beneath their boots. For two and a half days now they had walked and slept, then rose again and started over. Knox was cold in a way he had never been before, colder than he had ever even imagined. At least his magic still worked to create fires and move stones so that each night, they ate a warm supper, then made a bed nestled above the warm rocks.

So much had passed in the last few days. So much had passed in the last few weeks, and it shook Knox to realize how accustomed to Cailean he had grown. He was still gruff and stoic, still quick to temper and slow to smile, but he was smart, brave, good, and when he had lain under Knox's cheek the night before and carded his fingers through Knox's hair, Knox had pressed in close and pretended none of this was happening. They weren't two men on a death march into the frozen wasteland of Ailis's northern mountains; their mission wasn't almost certainly doomed to failure. They weren't two men held together by the single force of their forward trajectory into war and were instead simply two men finding comfort and pleasure in one another's arms.

It startled Knox to realize how easy it was to pretend.

111

Scared him how much he wanted to keep pretending.

But then the morning came, bringing with it the bitter cold of reality, and with each step that carried Knox farther from the simple life he'd had in Darry, the closer he came to the inevitable truth that things would never be that simple for him and Cailean.

"Cairn," Cailean said, coming to a halt.

Before them, deep in the valley of the frozen mountain they'd just trekked around, stood a sprawling settlement drenched in pale sunshine and blinding snow. Newer homes were built among the Old ruins: small, square houses with multiple chimneys from which curls of smoke drifted into the sky and disappeared in the weak sunlight, carrying with them the scents of pine and charred meat.

"Tides," Knox heard himself say.

"Come on."

They made quick work of the last few miles. Knox had been close to dozing off as they walked, his feet heavy with frozen mud, but now a new wind quickened their feet as this leg of their journey drew to a close. Neither of them spoke until suddenly, with a flurry of sound and powered snow thrown into the sky, four figures appeared between them and the village. They closed quickly.

"Behind me," Cailean said, and Knox wasted no time arguing. He flung himself behind Cailean's body, heart threatening to beat right out of his chest as the Mac Tire ate up the distance between them. "They will recognize my scent soon, but in case they don't—"

"They will," Knox said, feigning a certainty he did not feel and clinging to Cailean's shoulders.

It happened like something out of a dream. One moment the world was in sharp relief, the dark hair and dark woolen clothes of the Mac Tire cutting vividly against the white snow they kicked up as they closed in on Knox and Cailean at a furious pace.

The next moment, Knox was on his ass in the snow and Cailean was at the center of a pile of laughing and shouting Mac Tire. Their voices were too excited for Knox to catch any individual threads. They shouted over one another as Cailean dragged each of them in in turn, cradling their heads in his palm and rubbing his cheek against theirs.

"Um," Knox said, when it seemed no one had noticed his presence. "Hello."

Silence fell on them. One of the Mac Tire—an enormously muscled man with a shaved head and a thick red beard—turned and, upon seeing Knox, squatted down beside him in the snow. He peered at Knox carefully, as though Knox was a horse he was considering making an offer on.

"Highness?" he said after a moment in which Knox thought the man might pry open his mouth and check his teeth.

"Uilleam's son," Cailean replied.

The man sat back, balancing on his heels and letting loose a low, impressed whistle. "The Magus. He should come quickly, then. We've a need."

Knox was too tired to do anything and much, much too tired to do anything quickly. He considered taking Cailean up on that offer of being carried, but after a moment spent warring with himself, Knox decided his dignity wouldn't withstand the beating. He pushed himself to his feet.

The others took a step back.

"Don't mind them," Cailean murmured. "They don't see much of humans, and the ones they do… well."

"The Council's soldiers?"

Cailean did not reply, but the tense jut of his chin was answer enough.

"What need have you for the Magus?" Cailean asked, finally remembering himself and placing his body between Knox and the other Mac Tire. Knox barely managed to not roll his eyes. Surely if any of them was going to try something, the best time would have been when he was flat on his back and Cailean was in the middle of a group hug.

The man with the beard jerked his chin back toward the village. "It's Eileen's baby."

Cailean's entire body stiffened. "What of it?"

"She's come," the man said. "Only, she's early."

"How early?" Cailean said sharply. Then he froze. "It's a girl?"

"A girl," he replied. "They've called her Alexa."

"Alexa," Cailean breathed. "That's beautiful."

"And she's only a bit early. A few weeks, really. But... but she is early, Highness."

"Knox will come, won't you?" Cailean asked, grabbing Knox's arm. "Won't you?"

"I—of course," Knox answered. His head hurt from the sun and the exhaustion and the whip-quick conversation going on around him. "But what can I do?"

To Knox, Cailean gave no reply. He turned to the others and said, "Take us to her."

If Knox had thought traipsing after Cailean around the mountain was rough, trudging through the thick snow that blanketed Cairn was a thousand times worse. He tried to keep his head down, but the other Mac Tire seemed fascinated with him, walking too closely and peering at him openly. More than once Knox stumbled when he glanced up and found one of the Mac Tire inches from his face, gazing at him in wonder.

There were two men and two women. All four were huge, with muscles that bulged under their clothes and shoulders so broad Knox shrank down under their inspection.

"Aaron," Cailean said. "What of the Bringer?"

Aaron paused. "Katrina."

"Tides," Cailean swore. "I thought I made it perfectly clear—"

"Katrina does only as she pleases, Highness," one of the women said. "And you know you have no authority to tell her whom she may Bring for."

"How bad off is she?"

"It's still hard to say, Highness. Eileen and Viktor are looking after her as well as they may, but—but I think it's bad, Highness."

They reached the edge of the city and were met by more and more Mac Tire, who poured out of their houses and into the cold. Cailean did not stop to meet them, but he nodded at them as he followed Aaron. They nodded back, some of them openly crying. A few men had lifted small children and placed them on their shoulders.

"You see?" one man said, bouncing the tiny little girl balanced on his shoulders. "That's his Highness."

"The Phela prince?" the little girl asked. "Is he really real?"

"Of course he is," the man replied. "That's him right there."

They turned down a side street, leaving the chattering behind.

"We will leave you, Highness," Aaron said. He made a low bow and the others followed suit. "I pray you save your blessings for the child."

"It is as you wish," Cailean said.

"What was that?" Knox asked. "They were looking at me like children with a new bauble."

"They've never seen a human before."

"Well I'm not any different than they are."

Cailean stared at him. "Really? No different than the beasts?"

Knox rolled his eyes. "Oh, shut up."

The inside of the house was as hot as a furnace. Knox gasped as they walked inside, suddenly suffocating under the layers of wool draped around him. Cailean did not notice, but moved forward into the house. He turned down a hallway and rapped on the doorframe of one of what appeared to be a bedroom. A low, wide mattress took up most of the space, and someone had hung curtains of the cheeriest, sunniest yellow Knox had ever seen over the windows.

A young woman sat on the mattress, a tiny bundle of blankets swaddled in her arms. Beside her slept a young man whose face was shaded with exhaustion even as he snored softly into the pillow stuffed beneath his face.

"Eileen," Cailean said quietly.

The woman looked up and smiled. "I heard you. But I didn't want to wake Victor. He's been with Katrina for hours."

"Is this Alexa?"

Eileen's face lit up. "It is," she said. "She is well, Cailean. Katrina did not Bring when she should have. She kept her so

115

long, longer than she should have, and she was two weeks early anyway. Katrina is… she's not well, Cailean."

From his spot in the doorway, Knox watched the conversation in utter confusion.

"We're grateful," Eileen whispered. "So very grateful. But I feel terribly guilty."

Cailean stepped into the room and knelt, laying his hand on Eileen's head. Fat tears welled up in her eyes and rolled down her cheeks. "You know Katrina," he said. "And she doesn't do anything she doesn't want to do."

In another moment, Knox might have been amused by Cailean taking this advice given to him and turning it around on another person, but as it was, he could hardly think, let alone speak. Who was this Katrina, and why was she so unwell? The thought sat miserably in his chest, pressing at his ribs so hard he thought they'd shatter under it.

"Is she asleep?" he blurted out finally. "This Katrina, is she asleep?"

He had no idea why he'd asked the question, only that it was the right question to ask. Eileen looked up at him with surprise on her tear-stained face, as if until that moment, she'd had no idea someone else was in her house.

"She's in and out," Eileen said finally. "Cailean? Who is this?"

"Knox," Cailean said. "This is Uilleam's son."

Eileen sucked in a breath and looked at Knox with fresh eyes. "You are Shea's boy."

Knox startled, his grip on the doorframe going tight. "I am."

Eileen bent her neck, pressing her head to the bundle in her arms. She rocked back and forth, murmuring to herself, and after another moment, standing awkwardly half-in and half-out of the room, Cailean rose to his feet and motioned Knox out of the room.

"What was that all about?" Knox asked as Cailean pulled the door quietly shut behind them.

"We must see to Katrina," he said. "Rather, you must."

"And do what? I've no idea what's happening."

"Katrina is a Bringer," Cailean said. "She Brought Eileen and Viktor's daughter, but it is so hard to Bring a child like this. There is so little magic in these mountains."

"Bring?" Knox whispered furiously. Cailean stepped down the hallway and cracked open another room. "What does that mean, Bring?"

"Bringing is a magic I do not presume to understand," he said softly. "The Bringers, somehow they know when their magic is prepared for a child. There is a mating between the parents and the Bringer, and from that, a child is Brought."

"To whom does the child belong?"

"To all of us. It is birthed from the Bringer, but each of our children is a gift. Especially in times such as these, when the magic that sustains us is so very weak.

"It is why we must make our stand now, Knox. Do you understand? Our numbers shrink and shrink, and fewer babies are Brought. We are dying."

Knox nodded and touched Cailean's arm. Cailean smiled softly, swung the door open, and stepped into the room. It stood in stark contrast to the bright room where Eileen sat and held her sleeping daughter. This room was dark, with a tiny window high above the bed that brought almost no light through its opening, and eerily quiet. There was a stifling, unsettling quiet in the room that made Knox recoil. He fell back a step, then another, pressing his hands over his eyes.

"Knox?" Cailean said. It was only when Knox looked up and found Cailean hovering uncertainly in front of him that he realized he'd fallen to the floor and was crumpled in a heap in the corner.

"She's magic."

Cailean frowned. "Of course she is."

"No," Knox said. "She's a certain kind of magic. She's Elemental. A Bringer, you said."

"She Brings life," Cailean said. "She is chosen to Bring life."

"Move her," he said immediately. There was no time for him to fret or feel embarrassed or question why he knew what he knew. If he was going to save Katrina—and he was going to save her—she had to be moved now. But Cailean was shaking his head and drawing away, arms crossed over his chest.

"No," he said. "Absolutely not."

"She must be moved. She cannot stay in there, shut up like that. It's killing her."

"She'll have lost too much magic in her pregnancy, Knox. She needs time to recover. If we move her now—"

"I don't care!" Knox said, flying to his feet and pushing into Cailean's space. Down the hall, the baby burst into screams and wails. Cailean winced, but Knox did not even flinch. "She needs to be outside. She needs the air. The magic cannot get to her, and if it cannot get to her, she cannot heal."

"The cold will kill her, Knox. Look, I know you want to help, but Katrina never should have Brought this child. She knew that. She knew the risk she was taking. The last time—"

"I do not give a rising tide about last time," Knox shouted. His voice was shaking; every second he stood here arguing with Cailean was a second Katrina didn't have. Knox was crazed with it, beyond himself as he screamed and raged into Cailean's face. "If you do not move her outside and into the light right now, I will tear down the wall of this house and bring the light to her, I swear on my father's life I will."

The very air around them crackled with Knox's magic. Knox did not care that he sounded crazy. He did not care that he had woken a sleeping baby. He did not care that he was screaming at a man who could kill him with little more than a thought, or that he was surrounded by countless more who would happily do it for him.

"I swore my magic to you, Cailean," Knox said. "Let me use it in your service."

Cailean did not thaw; he ruptured. He grabbed Knox by the elbow and swung him around, slamming him into the wall. "If you're wrong—"

"I'm not," Knox said. He was certain of it, even if he had no idea why.

"Then open the front door for me."

Knox ran. He flew down the hall and threw open the front door just in time for Cailean to come barreling through, holding the limp figure of a woman in his arms. Knox's magic flared golden in his chest. He had to clench his hands into fists to stop himself from reaching out and snatching her away from Cailean.

Everything about it was wrong. The woman, this Katrina, she was meant to be full of magic, to overflow with it. Her skin was meant to be alive with the crackle of it, and her laughter was meant to float on a cloud of it. Instead, she was empty, a dried up husk waiting to be swept away on a strong breeze. Her very soul was empty.

"Put her down," Knox said.

Cailean looked at him with wide eyes. "In the snow?"

"I don't care," Knox said. "Just put her down."

Cailean hesitated, but then he knelt and carefully laid the woman on the snow at Knox's feet.

"Katrina," Knox said. He knelt down and touched her pale skin, which was covered in a fine sheen of sweat. She did not tremble in the cold, even though she wore nothing more than a thin cotton shift that ended around her knees. Her stomach was still swollen from her pregnancy. "Katrina," Knox said again. "Can you hear me?"

Katrina did not answer, just shifted her head restlessly against the snow.

Without rising from his knees, Knox reached out, pushing his hands through the air in front of him. It was easy, so easy he didn't even have to think about it. The magic came to him almost unbidden and curled up into his palms like a sleepy kitten. He gathered more and more of it, calling it unto him them, drawing it from the frozen pines and the hard earth and even the air that whipped around them, because Katrina was weak beneath him and Knox would not let her die. He turned his face toward the sun, growing the curls of magic into mighty fistfuls of power.

Then he leaned over Katrina and pressed his hands to her abdomen, pushing with all of his might. The magic hurtled through him, white hot and blinding. It poured out of his hands and into Katrina's body, and she accepted it like rain on dry earth, soaking up every last bit.

Knox had no idea how long they stayed like that, only that when he finally pulled away, he was shaking with the cold. He wrapped his arms around himself, shivering. Beneath him, Katrina opened her eyes.

"Magus," she said hoarsely. "Welcome."

TEN

"WHAT," CAILEAN said, snapping the door shut behind him, "the hell was that?"

Eileen's house was quiet around them. Katrina had been carried—over her vehement protests—back to bed, and Eileen and her husband had disappeared into their bedroom with a sleeping Alexa in tow, leaving Knox and Cailean alone in the low-ceilinged sitting room. The heat that had seemed stifling such a short time ago was welcome now; Knox dragged the blanket around his shoulders up higher and melted toward the fire.

"I don't know," he said finally. "I have no idea."

"You healed Katrina. You shouldn't have done that."

Knox looked up sharply. "I should have let her die?"

"No," Cailean said, sinking down on the couch and rubbing his temples. "I mean, you shouldn't have been able to heal her. For a Bringer to Bring a child early, they don't survive it. Not ever. It is the magic that binds the baby to them, and the only way they can Bring a child early is when their magic runs out."

To that, Knox could give no response. His head throbbed and his hands shook, even as his magic licked his aches, easing his pain. He knew with a certainty he couldn't name that Katrina was well and that she would remain that way, but the desire to see her and put his hands on her—to make sure Ailis's magic had settled back into Katrina's bones—pressed in on him.

"Start at the beginning," Knox said. "Please. I don't know what—what is a Bringer?"

Cailean tipped his head back and exhaled loudly at the ceiling. He stayed silent for so long that Knox grew restless and shifted uncomfortably under his heavy quilt.

"If you don't trust me, Cailean, this is never going to work."

"I do," Cailean said, meeting Knox's gaze with a firm one of his own. "I do. I just… this is magic I know little of, Knox."

"So tell me what you do know. Please."

Cailean cast around wordlessly for a moment, then shook his head. "Mac Tire are born of magic, do you know that?"

Knox lifted his hands in a helpless gesture. "You'd have to be, wouldn't you?"

"Bringers are… I don't know how to explain it. The conduit for that magic. Our babies do not come as yours. Not all Mac Tire women can conceive children, and not all Mac Tire men can father them. It's only Bringers who are able to harness the magic and Bring forth children. The birth of a baby, for us, it's…." He trailed off and shook his head, looking away from Knox. "It's a miracle. When my eldest brother was born, it is said the entire kingdom danced in the street for a month, drunk on honeywine and happiness."

Cailean's voice was so quiet in that moment that Knox felt guilty for intruding on what was clearly a private thought to him. He rubbed his cheek with the back of his hand and turned to watch the fire lick the sides of the hearth.

"My mother was a Bringer," Cailean said quietly. "It was unheard of for royalty to Bring their own children, but she was pregnant with my brother within a year of my father taking the throne." His mouth grew pinched then and his voice bitter. "They said it was a blessing from the fates that they should be able to conceive and Bring their own children, and so many at that. That it was a sign of a long and prosperous reign. Not quite, was it?"

"So Katrina, she Brought the child for Eileen and Viktor?"

Cailean nodded.

"And it's magic that allows her to do that?"

"Yes."

"And the baby—"

"Alexa."

"Alexa was born early because Katrina's magic faltered."

"We told her.... This is a difficult magic to begin with, and it's grown even more volatile here, so far from Forradh. I have tried to discourage it, but the laws governing that are far beyond my rule. It's an impossible situation. Katrina almost died when she Brought a child for a couple last year. It was four months before she could leave the bed. The only Bringer who tried to carry a child after that...."

The words hovered in the air.

"She died?" Knox whispered.

"Yes," Cailean said. "The magic failed her."

"It didn't fail her," Knox said. "It left her. Katrina's magic was gone from her. How does that happen? How can magic just disappear?"

"So you...." Cailean looked at Knox desperately. "You just... healed her?"

"I didn't heal her. I just helped the magic find its way back into her."

The hint of a smirk danced on Cailean's mouth. He shook his head. "You truly don't understand how unusual you are, do you?"

Knox's cheeks went hot. He ducked his head. "So she'll be all right now, won't she?"

"If that unholy ruckus she was making when I put her to bed was any indication, she'll be in here any moment to show me exactly how 'all right' she is by beating me half to death."

"You did lay her down, half-dressed, in the snow."

"You told me to," Cailean said indignantly.

"I'm a Magus," Knox said. "We're an unpredictable lot."

Cailean rolled his eyes and stood up. "I need to go speak with the others. You should stay here, get warm. Eileen is an old friend. She'll make sure you're well taken care of."

"Oh," Knox said. He hadn't realized he and Cailean would be separating, though if he'd thought of it, of course they would. Cailean had much to do. Plans to make and provisions to gather.

They were to meet up with the rest of the Resistance in a few days' time, and not a moment of that could go to waste. Cailean didn't have time for sitting around by the fire with Knox. "Yes, of course. Perhaps Eileen has some of that coffee Rhys is so fond of."

Cailean smiled then. It was a genuine, unaffected smile, and it was so different from his normal, self-controlled stoicism or biting indifference that for a moment, Knox lost his breath.

"Thank you, for Katrina," Cailean said. "Truly."

Before Knox could think of an answer, Cailean had slipped through the door and out into the snow, leaving behind nothing more than a gust of freezing air.

KNOX WAS awakened some time later by the sound of dishes rattling around in another room. He pushed himself into a sitting position, almost surprised to find himself asleep on an unfamiliar couch with a quilt tucked around him. He dragged his hands through his unruly hair, digging his nails into his scalp to wake himself up.

"Sorry" came a soft voice. Knox looked over his shoulder and found Eileen standing in the doorway, holding a chipped mug. "I didn't mean to wake you."

Now that the world wasn't spinning out of control around him—or at least it was spinning at a more manageable pace—Knox was able to get a good look at Eileen. She was a tiny slip of a thing, with long blonde hair that shone in the fading light of the evening. She had a fine, thinly boned face that shone with happiness through her exhaustion.

"What time is it?" Knox croaked.

"Barely four. The sun sets early in the mountains."

"Blimey," Knox said. "Forgive me, I did not—" He gestured at the rumpled couch around him. "I did not intend to fall asleep in your living room."

"Please," Eileen said, laughing. "You could fall asleep in my very bed and I would scold anyone who so much as blinked at you." She tipped her face up. "You saved Katrina's life."

"I—" Knox rubbed his hand over the back of his neck. "Perhaps."

"No," Eileen said. "Not perhaps. Certainly. We knew it was reckless when she came to us and told us the magic wanted her to Bring a child for us. But we wanted a baby so badly. It was selfish. I know that. Don't think I don't know that."

Knox did not know how to answer. He shifted uneasily on the couch and plucked at a loose thread on the quilt draped over his lap.

"I'm sorry," Eileen said, laughing awkwardly. "I don't even know your name."

"Knox."

"Well, Knox," she said, walking over and placing the mug on the table in front of him. "It is unspeakably nice to know you."

CAIRN WAS built on top of the ruins of an Old city. Most settlements were built within them, using the walls that remained to prop up new growth, but the Old city under Cairn had been buried under snow and ice so that only the tallest towers were still of use. The bridges that swung overhead looked treacherous. Even now, they were covered in thick snow, and when the strong winds blew across them, they swung lazily back and forth, showering snow and ice down on those beneath them.

From the warm sitting room of Eileen's house, Knox watched the goings through the window with fascination. The weather must be brutal and unforgiving, but the streets—such as they were—were busy. Men and women hurried about, their heads ducked against the wind. They moved with purpose, not lingering in the way the people of Darry did, but they still nodded at one another when they passed, occasionally ducking under an overhang to exchange quick words and handshakes.

"His Highness will be with the Elders," Eileen said. She walked into the room with a plate of steaming food. Across her chest was a long length of thick cloth, wrapped around her middle several times and knotted at her shoulder. A tiny fist peeked up around the edge of the fabric. "Do you like frost crabs?"

"I have no idea what that is."

Eileen placed the plate on the table beside the couch. Knox frowned and poked at the blood red thing on it. It looked like an enormous, hard-shelled spider with legs as big around as Knox's thumbs. "What is this?"

"Frost crab," Eileen replied. "They're sweet. If you don't like it, eat the boiled potatoes. I'll bring you some fire wine."

"But—" Knox poked it again. "How do I eat it?"

Eileen laughed. "Like this," she said. She sat down beside him and showed him how to crack open the legs and pull the fragile white meat from within.

"Eat it just like that?"

"Just like that," Eileen said. "Here."

Knox hesitated but, not wanting to be rude, carefully placed the meat into his mouth. It fairly melted on his tongue. He thought he'd never tasted anything so delicious.

"Oh tides," he moaned, licking his fingers clean. "That's delicious."

Eileen grinned. "Local delicacy. I'll get you another one."

"No, please, this is plenty," Knox said as he snapped the next leg off the frost crab and attempted to crack it open. Instead of coming out a whole, like Eileen's had, the leg snapped cleanly in two, leaving a chunk of meat in each side. Knox frowned and peered into the hollow legs. "Um."

"Give it here," Eileen said. She smiled down at the sleeping baby cradled against her chest. "I'd better get used to providing food for another mouth, hadn't I?"

"Is she all right?" Knox peered over at her. He couldn't see much aside from a sliver of her pink face and the tiny fist curled under her chin. "I know I woke her up earlier."

"She's fine," Eileen said. "She went right back down. She'll doze all day, then keeps me awake all night. Here." She handed him the plate of crab, piled high with thick, fat pieces of the sweet meat. "Another?"

Knox could have eaten about a dozen. "I don't want to trouble you."

"It's no trouble at all. We fetch them out of the river out back. I've got a pot of them on the fire right now."

Three frost crabs later and Knox was no closer to figuring out how to open them without spraying flecks of the meat all over the place. From her spot on the floor, Eileen was doubled over as she tried to hold in her laughter. Alexa was dozing in a basket beside her, contentedly sucking on her fist, but when Knox pried one of the legs free and sent the crab's body flying across the room, Eileen lost it, bursting into peals of laughter that roused Alexa grumpily.

"Oh, Alexa," she said as the crab slid down the wall. "Baby, baby, baby." She scooped Alexa up and began bouncing on her toes, making soft shushing sounds.

"Sorry," Knox whispered, still clutching the crab leg.

Eileen shook her head. "She needs to eat anyway. I should have woken her two crabs ago."

"I'll take her."

Knox and Eileen turned; Katrina was standing in the doorway, her skin so full of brightness and light that Knox felt some tangled knot of tension loosen in his chest.

"Katrina!" Eileen said. "You shouldn't be up!"

"I'm fine," Katrina said, waving Eileen off. "Truly, I am. I feel quite my old self."

Eileen bounced the baby in one arm and motioned Knox off the couch with the other. "Are you sure? Wouldn't you feel better if you lay down? Are you hungry? Surely you must be hungry. You've hardly eaten in days. Let me fetch you something to eat."

"I've been lying down for weeks," Katrina said. "And yes, I'm starving."

"We're eating frost crabs," Knox said, sheepishly holding up the leg in his hand.

Katrina raised an eyebrow, throwing a look over her shoulder at the crab that was lying in a heap in the hallway. "I see that."

"I'll get you some," Eileen said. "Three? Four?" She thrust the baby at Knox and disappeared into the kitchen, and suddenly Knox was quite alone with a baby, Katrina, and a crab leg. He bit down on his lip and tried not to drop the baby. Her weight was more than he would have imagined from someone so very tiny.

"Can I take that for you?" Katrina asked, her eyes dancing with mirth.

Knox tried to hold out the baby, but Katrina shook her head and took the crab leg instead. "Didn't Eileen teach you to open them?"

"She tried. I'm a bit hopeless."

"Hmm," Katrina said. She looked at Knox, then down at Alexa. "She likes you," she said, peering in and running a knuckle down Alexa's downy-soft cheek. "Alexa, I mean. Not Eileen. Though I imagine Eileen likes you just fine. Look how content she is. Little darling."

Katrina wasn't wrong. Alexa had stopped fussing and was dozing against Knox's chest, curled into a little ball of warmth.

"She's like a tiny furnace," he said as Katrina opened the crab leg and dropped it onto the plate. "Like a little bundle of sunshine."

"Mac Tire babies run warmer than you humans," she said. "She'll be like that for years."

Knox could have happily curled up with Alexa on his chest and slept the rest of the night away. He couldn't have said what it was about the baby that was so comforting, but a comfort she was. A moment later, he was swaying her side to side, humming tunelessly at her.

"See? Happy as can be."

Knox looked up from Alexa and grinned. "I don't remember the last time I held a baby."

"You're a natural."

Knox blushed but didn't stop swaying. "How are you feeling?"

"Unaccountably wonderful. Whatever you did—and don't go over modest now, I see you shaking your head, but you know you're the reason I'm well again."

"Magic is the reason you're well again."

"Well, then, Magus," Katrina said. "Whatever shall we do with you?"

A moment later, Eileen came back into the room with two more plates piled high with frost crabs. At the same time, the front door swung up, announcing Cailean's arrival with a blast of frozen air. Alexa grumbled unhappily and Knox found himself curling around her, shielding her from the cold. She cooed and settled into his chest.

"Cailean!" Eileen said. "You're back!"

Cailean shut the door quickly, closing out the howling wind. The streets had grown dark behind him. "We'll gather again tomorrow morning. The others are sending out word to gather as many as can reach us by then." He raised an eyebrow at Knox. "Made a friend, have you?"

"She looks quite at peace with him, does she not?" Katrina asked.

"Quite," Cailean replied. "And you look well yourself."

Katrina sighed and rose from the couch, walking over to Cailean. She wrapped him up in a hug and squeezed him. "There's no use in being cross with me, Cailean."

When Cailean pulled back, his face turned thunderous. "I told you specifically—"

"Which you know you have no authority to do—"

"Not as your prince, Kat, as—"

"As what, Cailean? My friend?"

"Yes," he said fiercely.

Katrina shook her head. "It doesn't work like that."

"I know," Cailean said. He sighed. It was a sad, defeated sound. Knox thought that maybe he should pass the baby over to him. It would be hard to be sad or defeated with such a dear little bundle in his arms. "But I wish it did."

"Then you would be wrapped in wool and kept in a fortress under lock and key, wouldn't you? And then where would we be?"

"Who the blazes is this lot?"

"Viktor!" Eileen said, and they all turned to see the man who had been sleeping earlier had risen and was standing in the doorway in his rumpled clothes, confusion sketched across his face. "Look, Katrina is well."

Viktor, a small, squat man with a round belly and a headful of orange curls, looked over at Katrina in shock. His eyes went huge. "Blimey. How long was I asleep?"

Katrina laughed. It was loud and bright, an addicting sound, full of earth and wind, and Knox felt it warm him like the early summer sun. He found that he was gently swaying Alexa back and forth again, gentle like a breeze.

"Knox," Katrina said. "He healed me."

"Who the blazes is Knox?"

Knox sheepishly raised his hand. Viktor peered at him, head tilted to one side. He sniffed the air, then made a face. "Human?"

"Yes."

"Huh," Viktor said. "Where'd you come from?"

"Cailean brought him."

"Cailean? What d'ya mean, Cailean?" Then he froze, apparently noticing Cailean for the first time. He stared at him with wide eyes, all the blood draining from his face. "Blimey," he said, pointing a shaking hand at Cailean. "Blimey."

"Hello," Cailean said, lifting a hand awkwardly.

"Blimey. Your Highness."

"Oh for tides' sake, Viktor, call him Cailean," Katrina said. "Let's not inflate him any more than is absolutely necessary, hmm?" She grinned and swatted at Cailean. "He barely fits through doors as it is."

"Hold your tongue, Katrina," Viktor said, hastily trying to flatten his hair. "You and Eileen may have known him since you were Brought wailing into this world, but I've never clapped eyes on him before now! I'll thank you not to tell me what to call the prince in my own home. Cailean indeed. Blimey. *Blimey.*"

After a moment in which they all stood around staring awkwardly at one another, Eileen cleared her throat. "Would anyone else like a plate?"

They crowded into the kitchen, unearthing a few rickety old chairs so they would all have a place to sit. After no small amount of shuffling—Eileen refused to sit until she had made sure Katrina was comfortable, and Katrina refused the chair Eileen gave her so Knox would not be forced to sit on the wobbly, cobwebbed old stool, and Viktor refused to sit at all until Cailean had, and kept springing from his chair every time someone so much as shifted—they set into the frost crabs piled high on the table. Alexa was dozing in her basket again; Knox snuck glances at her when no one else was looking at him.

"Here," Cailean said gruffly, startling Knox out of his staring. Knox looked up and found Cailean nudging a mound of crab meat toward him.

Knox bit down on a smile. "Thank you."

Cailean nodded and turned back to his meal. Knox spent the rest of his flicking glances at Alexa, snuggled into her nest of blankets, and Cailean, who was cracking open his crab legs with a determination fitting a man staring down his own doom.

No sooner had Viktor ushered everyone out of the kitchen to wash up than Katrina yawned, sending Eileen into a flurry of action.

"To bed," she said briskly. "You're still recovering."

"I want to speak with Knox—" Katrina began, but Eileen and Cailean both shook their heads, herding her toward the back of the house.

"He's not going anywhere," Cailean said. "Are you, Knox?"

For the first time in weeks, Knox realized that for the moment, he was exactly where he wanted to be. "No," he said, "I'll be here in the morning."

"You see? And we'll not have the chair situation again," Cailean said. "Katrina, you're still healing. Keep your bed. Eileen, you and Viktor are exhausted. And besides, Alexa's cradle is in your room, and it's warmest in there. Knox and I will do fine in here."

"Are you sure?" Eileen asked, wringing her hands. "Let me get you some extra quilts. Or we could—"

"Eileen," Knox said. "We'll be fine. We've been sleeping on the frozen ground for days. Your sitting room will be a luxury, believe me."

Later, when they were curled beneath a heavy stack of blankets beside the hearth, Knox struggled to find words for the thoughts bouncing around in his head. These people, these Mac Tire, they weren't so terribly different from the people Knox had grown up with and walked side by side with his entire life. They laughed and ate, they loved their children, they honored their family. It sat heavy on Knox's soul, how wrong he had been about them and for how long.

"It's easier, isn't it?" he said eventually, "easier to hate someone if they're faceless."

Cailean rolled onto his side and propped himself up on his elbow. "What do you mean?"

"For me," Knox said. "For humans. It's easy for us to fear you when you're faceless monsters. But you're not monsters," Knox went on quickly, feeling Cailean stiffen beside him. "You're not monsters at all."

"Close your eyes," Cailean said.

The darkness hid most of Cailean's face from Knox, but he did as Cailean bid him. The fire danced behind his eyelids, crackling and popping.

"Now open them."

Knox let his eyes drift open and found Cailean sitting beside him, teeth elongated, ears tipped with points and edged with thick black fur, eyes flashing golden. He held up a hand and showed Knox how his fingers were tipped in claws that would have pierced the strongest armor.

Knox should have been scared. He should have been terrified, but all he could think, as the breath left his chest, was how beautiful Cailean looked to him in that moment, how vulnerable he was, asking Knox to despise him.

"Still think that?" Cailean asked softly.

Knox reached up, carefully threaded his fingers through Cailean's, and told him, "Yes."

132

Cailean pressed forward and kissed him gently. "What do you want?" he whispered.

Knox went up on his knees and wrapped his arms around Cailean's shoulders. "You," he told him. "Just you."

ELEVEN

THEY WERE awoken by the sounds of Viktor prattling about the kitchen and grumbling, "The prince asleep on my floor, I ask you. I've never before in my life. Might as well have the ground crack open under my feet and give myself up to the Otherworld, hadn't I? Blimey."

Cailean groaned and stretched, knocking his legs against Knox's. "You'd think he'd natter about a bit more quietly," he said. "If he's so concerned for my rest."

Knox rubbed his eyes and rolled over onto his side, so that the length of his body was pressed up against Cailean's. He was careful, mindful of any move Cailean might make to show that now that morning was here, Knox no longer had the liberty of touching Cailean with ease. But Cailean simply responded by hooking an ankle over Knox's feet and tugging him closer. Their movement dislodged the quilts drawn tightly around them, letting the cool morning air skirt in and chill their skin. Cailean caught the edge of the blanket and pulled it back up, tucking it around Knox's shoulder.

Knox propped his cheek on Cailean's shoulder and buried his grin in the warm skin there. "I think this is the first time I've seen any of you sleep more than half a dozen winks."

"We can go longer on less sleep than you, but that doesn't mean we like to be woken any more than anyone else," Cailean said. His voice was gravely and thick with sleep. "It's hardly morning."

"If that. The sun hasn't begun to rise."

"You're not used to the sun's passage this far north. Short days. The sun rises late and sets early."

"Mmm," Knox said. He nudged his knee against Cailean's thigh and, when Cailean shifted to make room for him, slipped his leg into the warm space between Cailean's. It was intoxicating, pressing up against another body in so many places, being held so close. The arm that Cailean slipped under Knox's shoulders was heavy around him. Cailean's hand made lazy circles on Knox's back. Knox almost wished they hadn't dressed last night, after. He wanted to feel all of Cailean against him. Even though he'd only known him for a few days, Knox could tell that this ease and quiet didn't come often or easy for Cailean, and he couldn't bring himself to bring up Brae or Cathal or Pol now. Not in this place. Not like this. He snuggled in closer and ran his hand down Cailean's stomach.

They dozed then, breathing sleepily into the space between their bodies, only to be woken some time later by Alexa's hungry screams. Eileen appeared with her, bouncing her on her hip and stumbling into the kitchen.

"Sorry," she mumbled. She shut the door behind her, shushing Alexa as she went, but Cailean was already sitting up, pulling out of Knox's arms. The covers fell completely away as Cailean pushed himself to his feet and ran his hands through his hair.

Without another word, he turned and followed Eileen into the kitchen, leaving Knox to sort out their makeshift bed on his own. He folded the blankets and piled them in the basket by the hearth, trying not to feel disappointed by Cailean's casual dismissal. This was the way of things; Knox knew that. He and Cailean were little more than warm comfort to one another. A distraction in the rare moments they could afford it.

"Hungry?" Eileen asked, poking her head back into the living room. Knox turned and found her holding a steaming bowl in one hand, a chipped mug in the other. "You should eat. You've a big day ahead."

"Have I?" Knox asked, moving to relieve her of dishes, smiling when he realized the dark liquid in the mug was coffee.

"Cailean said you're going with him to meet with the Elders?"

The tension that had been tightening in Knox's shoulders lessened a fraction, then another when Cailean came back into the room holding his own bowl. Alexa was cradled in the crook of his arm. "Oh. Right."

"Might as well," Cailean said. "As long as you're here."

It wasn't an emphatic endorsement, but it was the closest Knox was likely to get. Under a blanket of stars and moon, Cailean was a man who craved touch. But in the waking hours, he was a prince with a displaced kingdom and a battle to plan. He obviously didn't possess the time or inclination to pander to Knox's silly emotions. It was stupid to get tangled up in the idea of him anyway.

Moving forward, that was where his focus had to be. Onward to Whit and then to Cahircluain.

"If you want me to," Knox said.

"Might as well," Cailean said again, and he handed the baby over and sat down on the couch to eat.

THEY TOOK their leave of Eileen and Viktor's house midmorning, bundled up in cloaks and scarves though the assembly hall where they were meant to be meeting was only a few hundred yards down the lane. The wind outside was bitter.

"Here," Cailean said, offering Knox a wide length of heavily knitted cotton. "For your face."

"You want me to cover my face?" Knox asked. "Is this some sort of secret meeting place?"

Cailean rolled his eyes. "Cover your mouth and your nose, idiot. It'll help you keep warm."

"Oh," Knox said, and he took the cloth and tied it around his mouth, knotting it loosely. Cailean was right, it did help, but Knox was still nearly frozen through by the time they had made it inside.

"Tides," he gasped, pushing the door shut behind him. The wind rattled it against its hinges. "My eyes are nearly frozen shut!"

"Be grateful you're not here in the winter, human."

Turning, Knox found himself standing before half a dozen Mac Tire who seemed no more pleased to see him than they would have a poisonous viper. Perhaps a viper would have been more welcome, and certainly more easily dealt with. Two of the Mac Tire had their claws out, and their eyes were flashing golden at Knox.

"His name is Knox," Cailean said. "He is a Magus, and he is here at my request. Control yourselves, you fools."

The Mac Tire shrunk back, their claws melting away like thawing ice. All except one man, who was both taller and broader than Cailean, and with a wildness about him that made Knox shift uneasily. His dark eyes were hooded with thick, black brows that narrowed as Cailean took a step in front of Knox.

"Ren," Cailean said, inclining his head. "Well met."

"Are you?" Ren asked. "Short notice, wasn't it?"

"We're not exactly overcome with time here."

The growling that rose from the Mac Tire made the hair on the back of Knox's neck stand on end. He lifted a hand to touch the small of Cailean's back and had a split second to feel how tight the muscles there were coiled before Cailean jerked away from him and took a step toward the long table that dominated the hall.

"Let's begin, shall we?"

Knox followed Cailean into an inner room, which housed a long oak table surrounded by mismatched chairs. A long, narrow fire pit ran the length of the room. It had been lit and banked, and a few large hunks of meat roasted above it, spitting grease onto the glowing rocks below. Unsure of his place, Knox hung back as the others took their places at the table. Cailean sat with his back to the fire, facing the door, and the one he'd called Ren sat directly across from him. His eyes flicked quickly between Cailean and Knox, then back again.

"Knox," Cailean said. He jerked his head to the chair at his right, and Knox slid carefully into it. "These are the Mac Tire Elders. Each of them represents a sect of wolves, and they bring their concerns and triumphs before us all."

"Or at least we used to," one of the men said. "Until we were scattered like so many stones."

Cailean exhaled and looked at the man who had spoken. He was slight, narrow in his shoulders and older than any of the others there. He wore his age like a mantle, his long gray hair tied back in an ornate braid that hung down his back. His thin face made Knox think of a beak.

"Clive," Cailean said. "Must we rehash this? If we are to retake the city, we will need as many fighters as we can gather. Our population is dwindling year by year, and the best way to increase our numbers is by convincing humans to join us."

"I'm old, Cailean, not stupid. Doesn't mean I have to like it. We're stronger when we're together."

Cailean laced his fingers together and propped his hands on the table. "We were out of options."

Clive sighed, then nodded, sinking back into his chair. The argument seemed to have taken all the fight out of him, and Knox became aware, in a way he never had been before, how the magic swelled and ebbed around these creatures. He sensed it as he never had before, as though it was a tangible thing, something he could almost reach out and touch. The magic around Clive felt silver and cool.

Knox shook his head and looked away. Things couldn't feel like colors, not even magic. His head was going on without him again.

Ren leaned forward, propping his meaty elbows in front of him and jerked his head at Knox. "You've a good reason for bringing a human to this meeting, have you? Quite outside the way of things, bringing a human to the Elders like this."

Cailean's jaw clenched. "It is not yours to question my decisions, Ren."

"Aye, but it is," said another of the men. He tipped his head at Cailean in deference, but his eyes were hard and sharp. "If you're moving on the Council, we want to know our men aren't being led like pigs to slaughter."

"*Your* men, Pator?" Cailean asked with a lifted eyebrow.

"Our men," Pator replied. "We might have followed your father blindly, Cailean, but you've not earned that right yet. Besides, look where that led us."

The woman at Knox's elbow hissed in a breath. "Hold your tongue, Pator. You willfully defy your prince in front of us? Have you no respect?" She leaned around Knox to offer Cailean a bow of her head. Her thin gray hair was pulled back into a low braid at the base of her neck. She could have been someone's grandmother, but power still rolled off her in thick waves. Magic or no, Knox felt he'd be a fool to cross her.

"It's not defiance, Vera. Why would he call us here if he wasn't planning to answer our questions?"

"I called this meeting because I have developments to share, Pator. Not to seek your approval for a plan already put in place."

"Developments?" Clive asked. "Since last night?"

"I wanted to give everyone a chance to travel here. I do not wish to keep anyone in the dark regarding our plans."

"Oh, they're our plans now, are they?" asked Ren.

"My plans *are* our plans, Ren."

"Is that right? Well, good of you to make the effort—belated though it is—to keep us informed. Even those of us who aren't usually granted the luxury."

Cailean's jaw clenched. With his hands curled into fists in his lap, he was obviously caught off guard at being spoken to in such a brazenly disrespectful manner. Knox could not figure out how to ease his furor or indeed if he even ought to try. He glanced at Vera and found her cutting a glare at Ren that could have boiled water.

"What of these developments, Highness?" she asked, turning back to Cailean. The tension around the table cracked enough for Knox to draw a deep breath and lean back into his chair.

Cailean's next words made him lurch forward again.

"This Magus has sworn fealty to me."

A low murmur filled the room. "To you?" asked one of the Mac Tire who had, until then, remained silent. "Or to the Mac Tire?"

"To me," Cailean said. "And he is powerful indeed. He healed the Bringer who carried Eileen's child."

The murmur became a buzz. Those gathered cut deeply suspicious glances at Knox, but he could tell this news held a weight

139

over them. Vera touched her hand to the back of his fingers fleetingly. When Knox glanced at her, her eyes were shiny.

"Young ones are such blessings," she said. "Especially in times such as these. Katrina is honored."

"He speaks to animals," Cailean went on. "And he controls the Elements."

"Hang on," Clive said, cutting through the buzz. "That's legend, that is."

"I've seen it," Cailean said flatly. "More than once."

"More than twice?" Ren asked. "More than three times? How often has your little pet—"

"That's enough!" Cailean roared. He banged his fist on the table with such force the wood beneath it cracked. "You go too far, Ren."

"Too far?" Ren laughed. "Do I? And how far is that, Your Highness? Would you even know?" He shook his head. "No, too busy running, aren't you? Too busy retreating, saving your own pelt. Sending men to and fro to take this settlement, hold that ridge. And when they're shot down like an animal—"

"Your wife is greatly missed, Ren. Agnes was—"

Ren was on his feet so quickly the chair he'd been sitting in clattered over, skidding across the floor. "You don't say her name!" he screamed. "Don't you dare say her name!"

The room was thrown into confusion as Pator leapt to his feet and grabbed Ren's arm, and Clive stepped in front of Cailean and cracked his neck, his fangs lengthening, his claws deadly points.

"That is enough!" Cailean shouted, breaking free from the hold Pator had on him. "Ren, you will calm yourself."

"Or?" Ren growled.

"Or nothing. Your position here is tenable at best. Do not make me regret having sent for you."

"Sent for me," Ren scoffed, his face screwed up in pure rage. "You don't send for me. I go where I please, *prince*." He spat on the ground.

Cailean froze; the emotion—shock and anger and betrayal— fell from his face as quickly as a hammer fall. Knox thought his heart would burst right out of his chest.

"We're to meet in Whit in four days. You will send for every man and woman who is able. The Resistance will join us there—and I know, Clive," Cailean said, holding up a hand, "your feelings about the Resistance, but our numbers are not so many we can afford to turn away help where it is given. And you'd do well to remember that these men and women are risking their deaths, same as us.

"Knox knows the weaknesses in the ráth. With his help, we will slip through their defenses under cover of night and attack the city before dawn."

Knox shifted unhappily. He was still not best pleased with Cailean's plans to attack the city without warning. He could only imagine the bodies that would be piled at the city walls by noon. And perhaps the Mac Tire were well equipped to deal with the weapons the Council would deploy against them, but Knox was human. The best he had was a useless ability to speak with animals and a shaky and unpredictable grasp on Elemental magic.

Still, Knox had given his word and his loyalty. And no matter what else, the men in that city were responsible for Shae's death. They had taken Knox's mother, Uilleam's wife, and Knox couldn't walk away while men like that held Ailis in their palm.

He had finally found a hill worth dying on.

"How does he know that?" Pator asked. "I heard he was with the Council's men, looking for us. How do you know he's not leading us into a trap?"

"He's Shae Cane's son."

The room fell silent. "He isn't," Vera said. She gave Knox a searching look. "Shae's boy?"

Before Knox could answer, Cailean raised his voice above the din and said, "But if you'd all be more comfortable, he can leave us."

"Excuse me?" Knox said, craning his head around to stare at Cailean incredulously.

"You're dismissed," Cailean said, without even displaying the courtesy of looking at Knox as he spoke to him. "The required introductions have been made. Your usefulness has been made known. Your presence is no longer necessary at this meeting."

Only his pride, as well as the scene Ren had made earlier, kept Knox from storming from the room like a petulant child. He stood slowly, nodded at Vera, then walked from the room wordlessly.

The door thudded shut behind him, and the freezing wind stung Knox's cheeks. He barely felt it. He would not pretend to understand everything that had gone on in that room, but Cailean rapidly blowing hot and cold at him terrified Knox. The way Vera had looked at him when Cailean spoke of his mother, the emotion that had played across her face… it was clear that not all humans were disposable to the Mac Tire. Perhaps it was simply Knox who was disposable to Cailean.

And when the front door of the hall opened and Knox found himself face-to-face with Cailean, he could not choke down the feelings clawing at his throat.

"So that's my use to you?" Knox said, his voice shaking with emotion and cold. "I'm a weapon? A tool? As useful as a bloody ax?"

"I thought I told you to go."

"You…." Knox could hardly contain the emotion that stormed in his chest. For days now he'd done and been exactly what Cailean asked of him, and none of it mattered. None of it.

"You should see to Katrina," Cailean said, moving to brush past Knox, but Knox reached out, reckless as it was, and grabbed Cailean's arm.

"I swear to the tides, Cailean, the next time you tell me what I should or should not do—"

"You'll what, Magus?" Cailean asked. He shoved Knox up against the wall, knocking free a shower of snow and ice that rained down on them. "You'll what, exactly? You're here because I wish it. Don't forget that. Don't assume you know me."

Before Knox could do more than gape open-mouthed at the man who had moved so gently above him hours before, Cailean had turned on his heel and strode off to be swallowed up by the whipping snow.

Later, Knox would wonder how long he stood there in the cold before the door to the meeting hall swinging open startled him. He glanced over slowly, still unable to believe Cailean's behavior, and found Ren moving toward him with an easy grace that made Knox shift away from him. He felt, for the first time, what it was to be something's prey.

"Where's your beast?" Ren asked. The wind grabbed his tangled hair and tossed it wildly around his shoulders as he moved forward, caging Knox in. His eyes were bottomless pits of black, and his grip on Knox's shoulder was of iron. "Left you all alone, has he? Unfortunate, that. Being left alone can make a man quite mad."

"Ren—"

"Quite mad indeed," Ren said again, wetting his bottom lip with his tongue. Then, without any warning, his arm flexed and his claws slid cleanly into the flesh of Knox's belly.

Maybe it was the shock of it, or maybe it was that the cold had frozen his senses, but it took a long moment for Knox to realize what had happened. And when he finally did realize it, it occurred to him in a distant sort of way, as though he were watching it happen to someone else, someone far away. He looked down and saw Ren's claws piercing his stomach; then he saw the blood blooming bright red around them.

No. Not the blood. *His* blood.

Knox looked up shakily. Ren grinned at him and yanked his hand free as rivers of blood began to pour from Knox's wounds. Knox gasped, hands flying to his belly.

"Very shortly," Ren whispered, wiping his blood-soaked hand on his pants, "you will feel no more pain. If that is any comfort."

The frozen ground was hard beneath Knox's knees, but Ren was right. He hardly felt any pain.

TWELVE

THROUGH HIS haze, Knox heard shouting. He blinked up at the white sky as dark shapes crowded around him. One voice rang about above the rest, piercing him. "His Highness! Find the prince! It's his Magus. Find him at once."

Weight pressed down on Knox's stomach. He moaned and tried to roll away from the pressure, but his body would not obey his commands. Even the smallest movement seemed beyond his grasp. But as his body faltered, his mind raced. He thought of Darry, of his father, of the sweet smell of summer's rain and freshly baked bread, and then inexplicably of Rian, the tiny baby with the magic light.

The pain overwhelmed him all at once, and he cried out, trying to roll to his side and curl around the wounds but hands held him fast.

"Be still," someone said. "Try not to move."

"Ren," Knox managed. "It was Ren. He's...."

A moment later, a familiar shape appeared in Knox's vision. Knox blinked, and the outline shifted into focus.

"Cailean," Knox breathed.

"Knox," Cailean said, his voice as wrecked as Knox had ever heard it. "What—" He shook his head and looked down at Knox helplessly. "Oh shit, Knox."

A dark shape hovered over Cailean's shoulder. "We should move him inside."

"Don't touch him!" Cailean roared.

"But—"

"Fetch Katrina. Fetch someone!"

"Highness—"

"Go!"

By the time the person had gone, Knox's eyes had drifted shut. It was much easier than keeping them open, and more peaceful too. His rest didn't last long, though, before Cailean grabbed and startled him awake.

"Knox, don't you dare shut your eyes, you blasted fool. You keep looking at me, all right? What were you thinking, hanging about after I told you to go home?"

"I wanted—" Knox licked his dry lips. "I wanted to talk to you."

"I knew something like this was going to happen. I can't— Knox, I can't protect you if you don't listen to me."

"Protect me? I thought you were dismissing me."

"Knox," Cailean said hoarsely. He bent and pressed his forehead to Knox's, breathed into the space between them. "I could not dismiss you if the moon commanded it of me."

The pitch of the voices around Knox was too low. They rumbled into his chest and rattled up the length of his throat, making his eyes water. He tried to shut them, but Cailean shook him again, and Knox forced himself to look up again.

"Katrina is coming," Cailean said. "She'll be here any second."

Knox wanted to shake his head, to tell him no. Katrina shouldn't be out in the weather, not so soon after the baby. But he didn't have the energy, couldn't find the words. And before he could manage to capture them, Katrina was above him, her pale face swimming into focus.

"Knox," she whispered. "Knox, can you hear me?"

He nodded and somehow found the strength to lift his hands. He found hers—shaking and stiff with cold—and pressed them to his wounds. "It's in the earth," he whispered. "And the air. It's in everything. You just have to want it." He blinked hot, gritty tears out of his eyes. "You just have to call it."

KNOX WAS warm when he opened his eyes. The room he was in was bright and the bed beneath him comfortable. He braced himself automatically, but when the pain he was expecting did not come, he let himself sink down into the soft blankets.

"Katrina said you'll be weak for a few days. You lost a lot of blood."

Knox rolled his head against the pillow. Cailean sat, straight-backed, in a chair in front of the door. His arms were locked over his broad chest, and his face was a mask of stone.

Knox swallowed around the lump in his throat. "Hello."

"She said she used the magic like you told her," Cailean went on with a frighteningly even tone. He smiled, showing all of his teeth. They glimmered like pearls in the dim light of the room. "Took it from the earth, just like you said."

Chills raced up Knox's arms. How likely was it Cailean would play along if Knox shut his eyes and pretended to drop back into sleep?

"She seemed upset," Cailean went on in that deadened tone. It made Knox ache to hear. "That she wasn't able to do more for you."

"Katrina is made of earth and fire. I am mere flesh and bone. Besides," Knox said, forcing a smile to his face. "I'm a much better Magus than she is."

"And so much stupider!" Cailean burst out, flying off the chair and crossing the room in two strides. He fell to his knees and grabbed Knox's hand, squeezing it tightly. "What on earth were you thinking? Ren could have killed you."

"I thought—"

"I don't care what you thought!"

"You just asked—"

"Shut up!" Cailean shouted. "Tides' sake, Knox. Just shut up." He drew in a shaky breath and lifted himself up to sit down on the bed, never letting go of Knox's hand. He clenched his jaw, then lifted Knox's hand and pressed his mouth to Knox's knuckles. "You can't... do this."

"Cailean," Knox whispered. His heart hurt, his stomach hurt, and Cailean was squeezing his hand so hard Katrina was probably going to have to heal that as well. "I'm sorry, I should have gone. I should have listened to you—"

"No," Cailean said furiously. "*This*. I can't... I can't feel like this about you."

He slumped like someone injured. His great body bent forward, mouth clamped shut tightly.

It didn't matter; the words were already out, and perhaps it was selfish, but Knox wasn't going to let him take them away. It was right, in a bone-deep way that Knox couldn't understand, for Cailean to want him, and for him to want Cailean in return; he'd known it when he sworn his magic to him. This land belonged to Cailean, and its magic had made a home inside Knox, and damned if he was going to let that get away from him.

"Kiss me," Knox whispered. Cailean lifted and pressed his mouth gently to Knox's. He pulled back almost immediately, but Knox caught him with his free hand to the back of Cailean's neck. "No," he said. "*Kiss* me."

And Cailean did, moving and settling his body gently on top of Knox's. He touched him with timid hands that grew bolder when it was clear Knox wasn't going to shatter beneath him. Knox could scarcely move, but it was Cailean's strength far more than his own weakness that pinned him into place. There was iron in Cailean's grip, unforgiving, and it should have hurt, bruised and broken and shattered as Knox was, but he could only be glad of it, could only lie on his back and revel in the satisfaction of being so possessed by another person—by Cailean. When Cailean slid his hands under the waistband of Knox's pants and slid them down over his hips, no force in the world could have stopped him from moaning out Cailean's name and clinging to him.

"Let me," Cailean murmured, as if Knox had any plans to stop him. He nodded and eased his hips up so Cailean could undress him, which Cailean did, with hands too gentle to belong to any sort of beast. This was nothing like their hurried couplings of the past; there was no clumsy grasping for skin, no grunts of impatience. Cailean took his time, never lifting his eyes from Knox's. Knox wanted to linger in this moment forever. It was a power unlike any he'd ever known or imagined, having Cailean look at him so.

"You too," Knox said, which was all the encouragement Cailean needed. He nodded and pressed a swift kiss to Knox's ankle—Knox grinned at the gesture—and yanked his shirt over his head. His boots followed, then his pants. He stripped his own clothes off with none of the care he'd shown Knox, but Knox barely noticed. Cailean was real and there, and Knox wanted him with a force he had never realized he was capable.

Cailean climbed back onto the bed, kneeing Knox's legs apart. He situated himself between them, then slid his hands up Knox's thighs.

"Look at me," he said, wrapping one hand around Knox's cock. "Don't close your eyes."

So Knox didn't. He watched, half-lidded, as Cailean nudged forward until he was settled into the cradle of Knox's hips and lined his erection up beside Knox's.

"If you ever do that again," Cailean ground out, "I will kill you myself."

Knox shook his head; his hair made a soft scratching noise against the pillow. "You won't."

"I might."

Knox shook his head again and pushed up into Cailean's grip. The pleasure coursing through his body was incredible. He had the mad thought that he'd happily never move out of this bed again if only he could keep Cailean here with him, his hips snug against Knox's ass, his hand wrapped around Knox's dick.

"Don't close your eyes. Don't look away from me."

Knox forced his eyes open, forced himself to watch, and Cailean took him apart with his touch and his gaze. His touch was gentle but sure; fundamental, like a wave beating down on the shore. He held Cailean's gaze as his pleasure swelled, as sweat beaded at his brow and trickled into the hair pushed back from his forehead. And when Cailean cried out and emptied himself over Knox's belly,

Knox was helpless to do anything except screw his hips up, shoving his dick into Cailean's fist.

He stared into Cailean's bottomless eyes and bit down on the words swelling up in his chest.

I think I was made for you.

MAGIC SWIRLED through Knox's belly. The spark he'd known since before he could remember was now a churning swell of magic that healed Knox much faster than he could have thought possible. It didn't leave him unscarred and whole, the way it did for Katrina; the skin on his belly was puckered and pink, but he didn't bleed, and his energy returned much faster than it should have. Even so, Cailean tried to forbid him from going to see Ren in the morning, when he would be taken before the Elders.

"The lunatic who tried to kill you?" Cailean said. "I absolutely will not allow it."

"You can't forbid me from going," Knox said petulantly. He sat in bed, on top of the covers but still in the sleeping clothes Cailean had carefully dressed him in the night before. "Katrina will help me get there if you won't."

"Katrina will do no such thing."

"Should we ask her?" Knox said. If he knew Katrina at all, she wouldn't take kindly to Cailean forbidding Knox from going to face the man who had almost killed him. Cailean knew it too. He scowled, pinning Knox against the bed with his gaze as effectively as if he'd climbed on top of him. That, Knox wouldn't have minded. The glaring, however, he would have been happy to give a miss.

"Knox," Cailean growled.

"I won't even speak," Knox said, sensing Cailean's resolve was weakening. Either that, or he knew Katrina would help Knox down to the meeting, and he wasn't willing to risk Knox to her. "I swear I won't. I just want to see. I need to know why he did it, Cailean, please."

"Because he's mad, Knox. Because living on his own all these years has driven him crazy. He tried to kill you, Knox. What do you think is going to happen?"

Knox couldn't have said what it was that compelled him to want to see this man. This man who had nearly taken his life. Knox was quite sure that Cailean would see him dead. Tides, he was surprised Cailean hadn't had him killed immediately upon his capture, if you could even call it that. Ren had done no more than wander down the street to a nearby pub, his hands still coated in Knox's blood and his own arrogance. Then he'd ordered a mug of mead and waited to be apprehended.

Perhaps it was that Cailean wanted to do the job himself, and why on earth did Knox wish to see that? He didn't know, but it seemed right somehow that he should. He dropped his eyes and looked down at his hands. "Cailean," he said softly. "I need to. I need to see it."

Cailean sighed and propped his elbows on his knees, dropping his head into his hands. "I don't wish you to see me at my most savage, Knox. You know what's going to happen. Can you blame me for not wanting you to see that?"

Knox reached out and wrapped his hand around Cailean's wrist. He tugged until Cailean lifted his head. "It's no less than I would do," he said. "If someone tried to kill you."

Cailean threaded their fingers together and squeezed. "Well," he said. "You may well get your chance."

REN WAS being held in irons in the small box of a room in the hall where they'd met the day before. Two men stood on either side of the door; they were huge, burly men with enormous chests and thick necks. Cailean nodded at them and they nodded back, their faces betraying no hint at their emotions. Knox hated what they'd come here to do. So many of the Mac Tire had been killed or had wasted away here in these mountains, unable to access the magic that caused their hearts to beat. It was clear to Knox now that he had met these wolves and felt their magic. Katrina had nearly lost her life over it. Their numbers were shrinking day by day, and now another one would die. Knox hated it. But there was no other way.

Cailean pushed the door open and stepped into the room. Knox followed, wrapping his arms around himself. A futile effort to protect himself. Not that he needed it. Ren was huddled in the corner of the room, sat back on his haunches. There was no sight of the arrogant man who had shouted in his prince's face the day before. Now he looked shrunken and beaten. Knox's heart shook when Ren looked up and grinned.

"Your Highness," he said, pushing himself up to his feet and bowing grandly. "What an honor to receive you here at these, my humble lodgings."

"Cut the shit, Ren," Cailean snapped. Knox tore his gaze from Ren and found Cailean had already shifted: his eyes glowed gold, his claws flashed.

"And you've brought your little pet with you, isn't that nice?"

Cailean growled and stepped in front of Knox. "Ren," he said warningly. Ren simply tipped his head back and laughed.

"Or is it the other way around? Has he brought you?"

He was trying to provoke Cailean. Knox couldn't imagine why. Fortunately Cailean didn't rise to his bait. He cracked his neck and retracted his claws.

"Ren Cowan, you are held here on charges that you did willfully and with deadly intent attack a human without provocation. You are also held on charges that you did willfully and with deadly intent attack a person under the protection of the esteemed household of your most honored prince."

Ren tossed his head back and let loose a chilling laugh. "I had a little fun with your whore, if that's what you mean."

Cailean's jaw clenched. "Do you wish to give your defense?"

"Where should I begin?" Ren said with a mad grin. "What would please you best, my... what was it? Most honored prince. Would you like me to speak of how you killed my wife? So I killed your bedmate? Or tried to, anyway." He licked his lips and turned his gaze to Knox. "What would it take for you to step inside and let me finish the job?"

Cailean's roar shook the walls. He was across the room before Knox could even blink. His fist closed around Ren's throat, and he lifted the man high in the air. His feet flailed and kicked uselessly above the stone floor. "Defend yourself," he demanded. "Tell me why, you miserable piece of shit. You knew… you knew you would drive me to this. Is this what you wanted, Ren?" He shook Ren, who thrashed uselessly against the wall. "Is it? Defend yourself!"

"Why bother?" Ren rasped. "It's death either way." He dragged in a breath and grinned crazily down at Cailean. "But it was always death, wasn't it? My most honored prince."

Perhaps it was fitting that those were his last words. Perhaps it was just. Without lowering him to the ground, Cailean heaved Ren away from the wall, then slammed him back into it with so much force that Knox heard his skull break. He was dead before his body hit the floor.

WHEN THE time came for them to leave Cairn, Cailean refused to even entertain the idea of Knox traveling with him. He bundled him into a covered cart with Katrina, who raged and shouted the entire time at being treated like an invalid; and Eileen, who held the baby in her arms and glared at Katrina until Katrina clamped her mouth shut and flung herself down on a stack of blankets.

"I'm complying under duress," she muttered as Knox folded himself up beside her. "Because Eileen will skin us both alive if we wake the baby."

"For my sake, I thank you," Knox replied.

They trundled slowly toward Forradh, stopping to gather up men and supplies. More wagons joined their caravan. Dozens upon dozens of wolves joined their ragtag group as they marched steadily towards Cahircluain. Knox liked to walk around while they were stopped to meet the others, all the while keeping an eye out for Cailean, who seemed as anxious to avoid Knox as Knox was to find him. Their last night together was an echo in Knox's soul. He played it over and over again as they crossed the rolling hills of Ailis.

A tangle of dread and hope filled Knox each time their wagon lurched to a stop, and he found himself both longing for word of his father and terrified of having any word at all. But none of the contacts brought news of him, and with Cailean giving Knox a wide berth, no one seemed eager to engage in conversation with a human, even if he was a Magus. It wasn't until the night before they reached Whit, a small, abandoned old ruin that had been left to the sun and wind, that Rhys joined them, bringing with her Anne, Yaara, and tales of Uilleam's fair health.

"He is on the outskirts of the ráth," she said, having gathered the Elders. They sat apart from the rest of the camp with their heads bent together over a fire Knox had summoned to cook Vera's dinner. Knox sagged in relief, freed, for the moment at least, from his burden of worry. Not even Cailean's stiff posture and refusal to meet Knox's eyes could tamp down the swell of joy that threatened to overwhelm Knox at the news. Yaara smiled at him and patted his arm. Knox found he was happy to see her. Relieved, even. "He and Jarlath are separating the Magi from the humans, trying to decide the best way to distribute magic through the ranks. There are some weapons. Not enough."

"How many are with him?" Cailean asked.

"A few hundred. Mostly humans."

Grumbles rose up from the Mac Tire gathered there; Cailean silenced them with a flash of his eyes and baring of his teeth. "Our numbers are not so great we can turn away help where it's to be found."

"I don't trust them," Clive said.

"I think," Vera said "that being Mac Tire is no sure test of loyalty to the crown. Ren proved that."

Knox pushed away the memory of Ren's lifeless body crumpling to the ground. He still could not allow himself to think about it, since relief was the only emotion he could find over it. "Ren was mad."

Clive let loose a bitter laugh. "We're all mad."

"The Magus...."

"I'll do exactly as Cailean commands me," Knox said. He glanced over and met Cailean's eyes; their gazes caught and held.

"He's sworn his loyalty," Cailean said. "He holds the Elements. There can be no defeat."

His tone belied his words. They were outmanned, outnumbered, and marching into a city with rings of defense against exactly this kind of threat. It would be a bloody miracle if any of them survived.

Still, hope was a thing that beat in Knox's chest even stronger than his heart.

"So...." Rhys said. She trailed off and looked at Cailean searchingly. Cailean nodded and stood.

"I've taken advice from the Elders"—he bowed his head respectfully—"from the Magus, and from my most trusted advisors. I believe our most honorable course is to petition the Council for the return of our lands."

Their voices rose up as well, shouting over one another so that Knox could hardly pick one voice out from the rest. Some of those gathered looked angry, others pleased. Josiah, the man who had replaced Ren, seemed too terrified to have any opinion at all and simply sat with his hands clasped, staring into the fire.

"They'll never agree to that—"

"—absolute madness—"

"—only position of honor—"

"—slaughtered, every single one of us."

"Enough!" Cailean shouted, lifting a hand and sending the others into silence. "If we descend upon them in the night and kill the innocents within those walls, we are no better than they are."

"No better? It's *our* land!"

"He's right. I cannot stand behind a king who would slaughter women and children."

"Cailean," Knox said softly. Cailean's gaze met his. Knox did not care how everyone around them went suddenly quiet. He could not look away. "Is this truly what you wish?"

"It is. If I wish to be an honorable king, I can't begin with the blood of innocents on my hands."

By the time the sun had set, their plans were set as well. Cailean would proceed south in the morning with a dozen or so of their strongest fighters and meet up with Uilleam and a contingent of magic users on the outskirts of the ráth. Knox had determined what he thought to be the weakest point, and through that they would cross into the city, hopefully undetected. If this diplomatic effort failed, they would fall back, Knox and the others providing what protection they could, and rejoin the others outside the ráth. Everyone agreed that, thus provoked, the Mac Tire would be within their rights to retake the city by whatever means necessary.

Rhys rose and nodded at Cailean. "I'll go to Uilleam."

"No," Vera said. "You've journeyed so far already. Rest. Let me go. Besides, it's been far too long since I've seen my old friend."

"You'll take someone with you?" Cailean asked.

"I will," Vera replied. She smiled at Knox. "I'll tell him you're well."

Knox nodded. "Send him my love. Tell him I long to see him."

He took his leave of them then, offering a tentative smile to Cailean and kissing Rhys's cheek, ignoring the rumble it caused among the others, and showed himself away from the clearing where they had gathered. Slowly, he made his way through from camp, where hundreds of Mac Tire were gathering for the evening, setting up their fires and sleeping rolls. A few people called out to him, but most simply ignored him.

"They have to know we're coming by now," Rhys said, falling in beside him. She tucked her hand into the crook of Knox's arm and followed him toward the place where Katrina had gathered three young children around a small cooking fire and was entertaining them with simple magic tricks. Something of the sweetness on their faces, the innocent and rapt way they watched Katrina pull shiny rocks out of their ears, tempted Knox. He sent out a flare of magic and laughed as a rabbit made of sparks leapt out of the fire. The children gasped and squealed. Knox grinned and released the magic, letting the sparks fall harmlessly to the ground.

"Again," cried one of the children. "Can you make a horse?"

"A dragon!" another cried out.

"Katrina!" Rhys shouted, Katrina gasped, leaping to her feet and throwing her arms around Rhys.

"Cailean said you were here! I was hoping I'd find you and look! Knox has led me straight to you."

Katrina smiled and nudged Knox with her elbow. "Ever so helpful."

Knox rolled his eyes at the pair of them and reached a thread of magic into the fire. He scooped up a fistful of sparks and shaped them into a horse, which he sent galloping around the circle of children. They screamed in delight and clapped their hands in glee.

"Now a dragon! Give it wings, Magus! Huge ones!"

Knox made one dragon, then another. It was easier than he would have thought. It reminded him of when he was just a young boy in Darry, sitting by the stream and calling frogs to him so that he could make them race. It made him think of Rian and his magic globes of shining light, and the joy he had in making them. Their lives were still so new and so full of wonder.

The dragons raced around one another on the breeze, flapping their golden wings and opening their tiny mouths. The children happily made sound effects for them, narrating the battle Knox acted out for them.

The sun was setting by the time Cailean found them, sinking down behind the gathering clouds so they blazed red and pink. He huffed a laugh and sank down beside Knox. "It's like a puppet show."

It crossed Knox's mind to ask what Cailean knew of puppet shows, but he didn't want to say anything that might break the fragile peace between them. It was clear to him why Cailean had pulled away. Before, the distraction they offered one another seemed like the easiest thing in the world. Now it was something each of them could ill afford. They would enter the citadel tomorrow and petition the Council for terms, something Knox was under no delusion the Council would agree to. Battle was inevitable, and Knox was overwhelmed with the idea of keeping both Cailean and Uilleam safe, not to even mention Rhys and Katrina and Eileen and the others. But for Cailean—every man and woman there was in his care, and with their numbers already so low, each death would be a blow to Cailean's heart. Knox almost longed for the simplicity Cairn had offered them. It had been a horrible place, and a horrible situation, but at least Knox had known Cailean was safe. At the very least, he had known Cailean was alive.

The children trickled back to their own camps when their parents called out for them. As darkness fell around them and the camp quieted, Rhys and Katrina wandered away, arm in arm, announcing they were looking for dinner.

"Sweet dreams," Rhys said, smacking kisses on Cailean's cheek, then on Knox's. Knox blushed and resisted the urge to rub his face on Cailean's shoulder.

The fire before them was dying away into embers. It was more of a challenge to bend it to his will, but not impossible. He gathered up some sparks and was shaping them into a crescent moon when Cailean leaned forward and, with a great rushing of breath, scattered them into the night sky like so many stars.

Beside him, Cailean shifted and then turned so he was facing Knox. In the gathering darkness of the evening, his face was nothing but planes and shadows, except for his eyes, which glittered. With careful hands, Cailean reached up and cradled Knox's jaw. He leaned forward and for a moment, Knox thought Cailean was going to kiss him. Instead Cailean leaned in so that his cheek was resting against Knox's. His skin was warm and smelled like pine needles and smoke and something spicy that made Knox breathe in deeply, filling his lungs with the intoxicating scent.

"Do you know how I knew you, that night in the pub?" Cailean finally asked, his voice soft in the quiet of the evening.

"I didn't know you did."

"I recognized you as soon as I saw you."

"How?"

Cailean nudged Knox with his shoulder. "I visited your father in Darry years ago. He'd sent word that the Resistance was gathering force, so I visited him there." In the dying light of the fire, his smile was soft. "You were so young."

"I don't remember that."

Cailean took in a deep breath. He turned and threaded his fingers through Knox's. He lifted their joined hands and turned them so he could press kisses to the soft skin of the undersides of Knox's wrists. Then he smoothed his hands up Knox's arms, up over his shoulders, up farther still until he was cradling Knox's jaw in his warm, familiar hands.

"I pray you safety," he whispered. "Long life. Happiness." His breath hitched as he smoothed his thumbs over the planes of Knox's cheeks. "Love."

Knox reached out, wrapping his arms around Cailean's waist. It wasn't much, but it was enough. It was more than. Knox closed his eyes and clung.

THIRTEEN

SLEEP USUALLY clung to Knox for hours after waking. Even when he was a young boy and the world seemed full of limitless opportunities to explore and play, Knox always had trouble forcing himself out of his bed until well after the sun had begun to warm the earth. On this day, though, Knox woke as though he hadn't been sleeping at all. Perhaps he hadn't been. It certainly felt as if he'd been tossing and turning from sundown until the very edge of sunrise, when the camp began to wake. He climbed out of his bedroll and stretched, wincing at the way his back muscles twisted.

He turned and found Cailean already standing some distance away, his arms crossed over his broad chest. In the distance, Cahircluain... no, Forradh. It was far past time for Knox to recognize the city by calling it by its true name. In the distance, Forradh rose from the early morning mist like something out of a dream, tall and proud and just out of their reach.

Almost as if he felt Knox's gaze upon him, Cailean turned and looked behind him, his eyes going directly to Knox. Knox sat for a moment and soaked up the sight of him: his pale cheeks, his dark, thick hair, the way his eyes were a million different colors all at once. For all his flaws, Cailean was a good man. He would be a good king. And the Mac Tire, these people who had been banished and made to live a frozen, nearly barren life, they deserved a good king.

Knox pushed himself to his feet and walked over to Cailean. He slid his hand into Cailean's and squeezed. "Let's go finish what we started," he said, and Cailean squeezed back.

Knox watched as Cailean moved through the camp, sharing a quick word here and there. He gathered up a dozen or so men and women to accompany them into the city. It was an odd group, but Knox had to trust that Cailean had reasons for his choices. He couldn't hide his surprise, though, when Rhys did not join their group.

"You're not bringing Rhys?"

"We can't both go." He handed Knox a pair of leather wrist gauntlets. "Put those on."

"But—"

"No," Cailean snapped.

"No what?" Rhys said, coming up behind Cailean with murder on her face. "You're not leaving me here, Cailean."

"You're not coming with us."

Rhys's eyebrows flew upward. "The hell I'm not. They're my people as much as they are yours."

"Exactly," Cailean said. "Someone needs to be here to... in case the worst happens."

"Which is exactly why I should go. You need all the good fighters you can get. I'm just as strong as a man. I fight just as well."

"That's nothing to do with it, Rhys, and you know it. The Council doesn't know about you. I'd like to keep it that way. I'm the one they want."

"All the more reason for you to stay here, stay hidden. You're the one they're kidnapping people left, right, and center to get to."

"Well they won't have to do that anymore, will they? Not if I'm delivering myself to them." Cailean wrenched his pack open and wrestled a leather breastplate out. He thrust it at Knox. "Put that on."

"Cailean, what—"

"You're not marching in there unprotected, Knox. If you want to go, put it on."

"Unprotected? But you'll—"

"Just put it on!" Cailean roared. The others gathered around them recoiled. Their fear was written large across their faces: if Cailean couldn't control his temper, how would he control his shifting?

"I don't think Knox should go," Rhys said, crossing her arms over her chest. "It's clear you can't control your emotions when he's involved."

"Hang on—" Knox began, because no force in Ailis would keep him from Cailean's side that day. But he got no further than that before Cailean reached out and grabbed Rhys's arm.

"Listen to me," he hissed. "They will not bargain with you. You mean nothing to them. I'm the one they want. It's the only play we have, Rhys, you know that."

"Cailean, if something happens to you—"

"If something happens to me, if we're not back by nightfall, you turn these men and these women around, and you march them as far north as you can. You take them into the mountains, do you hear me? You get as far away from here as possible, and you do it as quickly as you can."

It seemed the entire world around them had been snagged, caught motionless. No birds chirped; no man cleared his throat. In that moment, there was only the two of them and their desperation to save the only family they had left.

Knox blinked the grit from his eyes and turned away. He missed his father.

When he was able to look back, Cailean had Rhys's jaw cradled in his hands, his cheek brushing against hers. He whispered something none of them could hear—something none of them were meant to—then turned and nodded. "To Forradh."

By midmorning, they had reached the ráth and found Uilleam waiting with a small cluster of men and woman. Knox broke free and ran to meet him, his long legs eating up the distance between them.

"Knox," Uilleam said, reaching out and grasping him. For a long moment they held one another fast, heedless of the audience around them.

"You're safe," Knox said, holding his father at arm's length and examining him. His bruises had faded to a dull, sickly yellow. Uilleam chuckled and shook his head, and Knox ran his hands over his injuries.

"Quite," Uilleam replied. "I told you Rhys would look after me." He looked around, then turned to meet Cailean's gaze. "Rhys?"

"At camp."

Uilleam sighed but nodded. "I've brought half a dozen of the strongest Magi, as you requested."

Cailean jerked his head at them. Knox could have laughed at the craziness of it all. Twenty men and women, marching into a city fortified by an army of hundreds, fortified by dozens of Magi, and requesting that they be given freedom. It was madness, especially knowing the lengths the Council would go to in order to eliminate anyone and everyone who posed a threat to their rule. For a moment, Knox regretted insisting that Cailean try to reason with the Council. He was going to lead them all to their deaths.

He turned to find Cailean, to tell him to call it off and retreat back to camp, but Cailean met his gaze and shook his head sharply.

"You'll lead us," he said. "Show us the best place to cross the ráth unseen."

"Cailean—"

"The time for discussion is long past," he said. Then he lowered his voice, pitched it so the others could pretend not to hear it as he told Knox, "This is my decision, Knox. You were right. It's the honorable thing to do."

It was a warm day, and even more so after the time spent in the frozen mountains of Cairn. Under the leather of his wrist gauntlets, Knox's skin was damp with sweat. He shoved his hair off his forehead and nodded, drawing himself up.

"East from here," he said, calling to mind the maps he'd stolen from Cathal and copied down. "About three miles."

"Dawn can cast spells that will cover us."

"They're not flawless," a small woman piped up. She had short red hair and a smattering of freckles across her pale skin. "But they'll confuse anyone who should look too closely at us."

Cailean flashed her a look of approval and nodded. A rumble traveled through the other Mac Tire, clustered in a knot a bit away from the humans, and a few of them traded uneasy glances.

"We trust these people because...."

"Because we have no other choice," Cailean replied. "The magic is draining out of this land, and it'll continue until our kind are reinstated in Forradh. Uilleam has been working for the Resistance since before most of you were born. He wouldn't bring us men who were disloyal."

Knox, standing between Uilleam and Cailean, craned his head around to examine the Magi his father had chosen. His magic, which had been, for most of his life, a small cluster of threads in his chest, now felt like a never-ending blanket he could spread out at will, and he did so now, seeking out anything that felt wrong in any of those gathered. It was not unlike the way it had always come to him with animals, though much stronger now. A few of those gathered gasped and shifted, looking at him in bewilderment, but none of them resisted the magic, and none of them gave Knox any indication that Uilleam's trust—and Cailean's—was misplaced.

"To trust me is to trust Uilleam," Cailean finally said, once the silence had stretched to the point of discomfort. "We should move. Before we lose any more time."

It was with an uneasy rumble of noise that they began to move east. The Mac Tire clustered together and walked silently, their heads held high and chins jutted forward. Some of them were older and weathered; some of them were so young they likely hadn't even been born when Ailis fell to the Council. They were marching into the unknown, led only by their trust in the man who walked ahead of them. And just behind them, the human Magi seemed tied together, unable or unwilling to attempt to join the Mac Tire. They whispered among themselves, occasionally letting out a quick bark of laughter that was quietly hushed by a stern look and a cleared throat. At one point, a young man with white hair and the palest complexion Knox had ever seen complained of the heat; Knox called up a wind that rustled the dead grass at their feet and cooled the sweat beading their brows.

163

Knox adjusted his pack and breathed in the cooler air, trying to let it clear his mind. He muttered to himself, trying to think up any bit of magic that might be useful. If things went poorly, as he feared they would, they would need to beat a hasty retreat back to camp to gather the rest of their forces. Knox had never tried to speak to more than a handful of animals at a time, but if he had to, perhaps he could call upon the Council's horses to turn back or to refuse to move. As for the infantry and those who would pursue them on foot… a wind, perhaps? A sandstorm to block their pursuit. Assuming, of course, that he could control a wind well enough to only affect those men and not impede the Mac Tire's progress. A brief, horrible thought crossed his mind to use animals to attack the Council's soldiers, but his stomach turned as soon as the thought occurred to him, and he dismissed it immediately.

Before he knew it, they were turning south and heading toward the ráth. They had chosen a place that was barren and ill-equipped to sustain the camps of Magi the Council kept stationed there, and indeed, as they crept along, it was clear there were no camps and no patrols. But the magic of the ráth pulsed through the air, and Knox looked around wildly.

None of the others seemed to notice the change. The Mac Tire, who were themselves born of magic and whose bodies were nearly overrun with it, did not hesitate as they moved ever closer to the line of magic stretched across the land. The Magi, whose blood was meant to be thick with the same fire, stuck close behind them and chattered on, as if they were out for a picnic or a fishing trip.

"Hang on," Knox said, reaching out for Cailean's arm. "Cailean, wait."

Cailean stopped; the rest of their party lurched to a halt.

"Don't you feel that?" he asked. "Do any of you feel that?"

Cailean frowned. "Feel what?"

"The magic," Knox replied. "Can't you feel it?"

One of the Mac Tire shook his head and kicked up a dusty cloud. He spat on the ground and then rubbed his boot over it. "Can't feel nothing, Magus."

Knox took several steps forward, shaking his head when Cailean tried to follow. "Just hang on," he said, holding up a hand to stop him. He walked on, and as he walked, the magic became a steady thrum. It hummed like a string out of tune, casting a vibration over the land that was out of sync with the earth around it. Knox slowed his pace and edged onward, his hands curling into fists at his sides. Then, quite without warning, the stones beneath him crumbled so that Knox was forced to throw himself sideways to avoid the cavern that was cracking open. Knox hit the ground hard and rolled away, his heart banging around as he came to a stop.

"Knox!" Uilleam shouted, his voice rising above the thundering of the rocks cascading down the gash of earth beneath Knox's feet.

"I'm all right!" Knox yelled back, his voice shaky as he stared at the hole in the earth where he had stood moments before. He pressed his hand to his throat and felt his breath dragging in and out. "Tides."

"What the hell?" Cailean yelled. He was pacing back and forth on the far side of the ravine, his eyes completely mad. He tugged at his hair, making restless motions like he was going to charge up to the gaping hole. Luckily, Uilleam had him by the back of the shirt and kept him back. Knox, having absolutely no notion to move now he was on steady ground, forced himself to his feet and met Cailean's gaze.

"I'm fine, Cailean. Look. See?" He spread his arms out, biting back a wince as a muscle in his shoulder pulled.

"What happened?"

"The magic here," Knox said. He rubbed the shoulder that had taken the brunt of his weight, digging his fingers into the meat of his muscle. "Something's wrong with it."

"It was a trap," one of the Mac Tire said, and the others murmured their agreement. Their voices rose up even as Knox shook his head.

"No," he said. "No, this isn't—this is Old magic. This wasn't laid for us."

Cailean narrowed his eyes and shifted from one foot to the other. "You're sure."

"As sure as I am of anything," Knox replied. He couldn't have said how he knew, just that he did. He moved to the edge of the ravine, drawing a hiss from Cailean, and peered down into the darkness. The yellow of the sunburnt grass gave way to the brown earth below, then the muddied gray of the stones below that. The ravine was barely ten feet across but stretched out far in either direction. Knox shook his head and stepped back from the edge. "I can't do anything for it. You'll all have to go around."

"You'll show us where."

A few hundred feet east, they found the place where the crack healed, and the others were able to cross. The magic that had felt so uneasy to Knox was less here than it had been, so he nodded and indicated to the others that they could pass here. They went quickly, one by one, with Cailean bringing up the rear, until they were all on the far side of the gorge.

"How's your shoulder?" Cailean asked, coming to stand beside Knox and placing a broad hand on the nook of his neck.

"Fine," Knox said. He had to tamp down the urge to sink into the warmth of the touch, to turn and press himself into the safety of Cailean's body. His heart was still shaking behind his breastbone, and he couldn't understand what had happened, really. Why had the earth given way? And how had Knox known it would? "Barely hurts."

Cailean huffed a laugh. "Liar."

Knox did not answer and instead simply stayed close to Cailean's side as they began moving in earnest. Now that they were across the ráth, they sped up without any of them speaking of it or seemingly even making a conscious decision to do so. Knox forced himself to focus on his own feet and the ground they steadily ate away at, because all he wanted to do was press in close to Cailean and rub his mouth over the unshaven skin of Cailean's cheek. But it would not do to make himself so obvious, especially now. This close to Forradh, all of them were straining forward, hyper-focused on what was coming.

As they drew near to the city walls, a low cloud of dust appeared in front of them, followed quickly by the thundering of hooves. Cailean was quickly surrounded by the Mac Tire, who extended their sharp claws and cracked their necks, allowing their fangs to drop. Knox saw more than one of the Magi shiver at the sudden shift; he found he couldn't blame them. Committed as he was to Cailean's side, the sight was still terrifying.

Two riders appeared before them, the colors of The Council blazing on their chests. Cailean paused by a collection of old, gnarled tree trunks, and the others paused as well, assuming battle positions. They closed ranks, each person with someone at his or her back. Two of them dropped low, bracing themselves in crouches, the muscles of their shoulders shifting restlessly beneath their skin. Knox fell back, seeking his father out. And Uilleam was moving toward him as well, grabbing him by the arm and hauling him behind the Mac Tire.

"Father—"

"Wait," Uilleam murmured. "Just wait."

Cailean reached out and grabbed Knox's arm in a bruising grip. "If it comes to a fight, I want you to stay out of it."

"But—"

"Please, Knox," Cailean said. He squeezed Knox's arm. "I need to know you'll be safe."

"I—" Knox meant to fight back, but one look at the desperation on Cailean's face, and Knox was nodding before he realized it.

The horses closed on them quickly. Knox peered up at the men seated upon them, half-expecting to see Cathal or Pol and Brae, but both men were strangers. One was older and broader, dark in every way, down to his black eyes. The other man was much younger, with legs that seemed far too long for his body. He held the Council's flag aloft, one hand gripping the leather reins wrapped around his horse's neck.

"What's your business?" the younger man asked as he brought his horse to a stop in front of their group. The other man, half a length behind him, sucked in a breath and yanked on his horse's reins so quickly the horse whined and reared back.

"Beasts," he hissed, hatred and fear written large across his face.

The young man jerked back, nearly unseating himself. His eyes went wide, and he looked around wildly. "Tides," he said, dropping his banner and reaching for the bow on his back. Before he could do more than wrap his hand around it, Knox sent a coil of magic. The man's horse shifted quickly, making the man grapple for the reins.

"Don't even think of it," Knox said. "You'll be dead before you can notch your first arrow."

"Outnumbered, is it?" the older man asked. He narrowed his eyes at Knox. "You're that Magus, ain't it?"

"I am," Knox replied.

"Fall in with them beasts, have you?" he asked, grinning stupidly. Knox would have liked to knock the smirk right off his face. But assaulting one of the Council's guards would only make their situation worse, if such a thing were even possible. "The Seers said your lot was headed this way. Didn't reckon I'd be the one to take you in."

Knox jerked forward, but Uilleam stopped him with a hand to the chest and a quick shake of his head.

Cailean drew himself up. "We seek an audience with the Council."

"I bet you do," the man sneered. "Lucky for you we've got orders to take you there directly."

Knox bristled; he didn't much care for the sound of that. Of course they had anticipated the Council would be aware of their movements—their numbers weren't great, but they were too large for so much activity to go unnoticed—but the idea that they were prepared for the Mac Tire's arrival—that they had sent out men to hunt for them—was unsettling. But there was nothing else for it. If they turned back—something Cailean surely wouldn't agree to—at least one of them would be taken down by the Council's soldiers. No, the only way was onward, into the fray. Knox forced his feet forward, keeping his eyes trained on the back of Cailean's head, seeking comfort in the fact that he was surrounded by the best fighters they had. He wished he was close enough to put his hand on

Cailean—to steady himself, he thought, more than as any sort of support for Cailean.

Flanked on either side by the two soldiers, they made their way toward the city center.

GENTLE HILLS gave way to the wide, dusty road that unfurled through the city gates. They entered Forradh through the lower town, where crudely built wooden houses leaned against one another in long rows. Clotheslines were strung between the rows, holding faded and worn cloth that hung limply in the stagnant summer air. The first time he had come to Forradh, when he'd still known it as Cahircluain, he and his father were at the end of a pair of swords, and Knox had been too terrified to take in much of the city. Now he couldn't help but be overwhelmed by how dirty the place was, how poor and miserable the people seemed. They huddled in doorways and stared up at the Council soldiers with eyes sunken low in their chapped faces. Then their eyes slid to Cailean and the Mac Tire who surrounded him—Knox didn't think he imagined the hope he saw there.

They made their way through the city, past the guard towers that marked the inner wall surrounding the castle. One of the Magi walking near Knox stumbled as he shaded his eyes with one hand and peered up at the turrets.

"Tides," he muttered. "It's bleeding huge."

If any of the Mac Tire were affected by returning to their royal seat—if Cailean was affected by the place where his family had been slain—none of them showed it. Their faces were set, their resolve steely. Knox mimicked their posture and hoped that in it he would find that same determination. It wasn't easy, for the castle at the center of Forradh was a mighty thing that sprawled lazily across the land and climbed ambitiously toward the sky.

Through the courtyard they went, past great concrete statues, around the bushes dripping with fragrant flowers, and up the wide steps that led to the heart of the castle. An enormous gate hung high in the air, threatening to crush any who dared cross the bridge it guarded uninvited. Neither of the Council's men paid it any mind. They kept their pace steady and only dismounted their horses when they had reached the main doors of the castle. There they found other men waiting to escort them before the Council. Unsettled as any man could be, Knox hardly noticed Brae among the men who led them into the great hall. Brae glared at him with betrayal on his face, but Knox only had eyes for Cailean, who had stepped out of his circle of protection and was striding into the hall with so much authority that many of those standing nearby and gawking at the spectacle fell back with murmured gasps.

Knox gripped his hands behind his back, his lungs barely taking in air the way they were meant to. Shallow, unsteady breaths forced their way into and out of his chest. He squeezed his eyes shut against the dizziness that threatened him, then forced them open again.

A dais ran the width of the great hall, and on it stood a long, polished wooden table. Behind the table were six high-backed chairs draped in red cloth. Upon each of the chairs was seated a man dressed in finery beyond any imagining: thick, velvet cloth adorned their garments; golden circlets jangled upon their wrists; glittering gems dripped from their fingers. One of those gems could have purchased enough grain to feed the whole of Darry for a winter season.

One of the men seated at the table stood, and the murmurs in the hall fell silent. He was tall and thin, with golden hair that curled around his ears. A slow, lazy grin spread across his face as he held his hands out, palms up.

"Well," he said. "Welcome to Cahircluain."

If the slight—calling the city by its Council name, rather than the name the wolves had given it ages before—was meant to invoke a response, it failed. None of the Mac Tire responded, except perhaps to clench their jaws tighter, to curl their fists with that much more force. Knox thought it would almost have been a relief if they had taken the bait the man laid at their feet. At least this interminable waiting would be over. Knox never thought himself much a man of action, but this slow game was driving him into an absolute frenzy. Beneath his skin, his magic crackled and sizzled, tempting him.

Cailean took another step forward and tilted his head up to meet the man's gaze.

"I am Cailean Phela," he said. "The last prince of Ailis, and I've come before your Council to petition you for the safe return of my family's land."

The man's grin turned sinister; his eyes were black as coals. "At last," he said. "I am Angwyn. And the answer, of course, is no."

Angwyn jerked his head, and two dozen men, probably more, poured into the room from all sides. The sunlight filtering through the windows glinted off their weapons—swords and mauls and bows already notched with arrows. They were dressed head to toe in armor that rattled as they moved to surround the Mac Tire.

However frightening Knox had perceived them to be before, it was nothing compared to what happened now. Each of them let out a mighty roar that shook Knox in his boots. They moved with inhuman speed, lashing out at each man who came near them. The power in their blows was nothing like Knox could ever have conceived. One man charged at Cailean with a scream; before he could even lower his blade, a woman moved in front of him and grabbed him up by the throat. She threw him like a child would throw a ball or a stick for a dog to fetch. The man arched through the air and landed headfirst at Angwyn's feet. Even in the chaos of the hall, Knox heard the sound of his neck breaking.

Knox swallowed down the bitter taste that flooded his mouth. A moment ago, that man had lived, and now his life was over. How many more would meet that end before the day was over?

The clash of metal and the screams of the wounded and dying filled the air. Knox was knocked backward, into the other Magi as a blur of flesh and iron clashed around them. No sooner than one Council soldier hit the ground than another was there, taking his place and offering up his own life.

At that moment, a ringing tore through the room. Knox whipped around just in time to see a seax hurtling through the air. It moved too quickly, and its aim was true. Knox wouldn't reach

Cailean before it split his skull in two. He opened his mouth to scream out; the sound turned to blood in his ears as Clive leapt in front of Cailean and knocked him to the ground. The seax missed its mark in Cailean but found it in Clive. A look of shock crossed his face in the moment before the seax sunk into his throat.

He went down slowly—knees, elbows, hands—then all at once. His body hit the floor with a sick thunk. Blood poured out from beneath him, spreading out thickly on the polished marble of the floor.

The sight of the blood, or maybe it was the scent of it, or maybe it was both, sent the Mac Tire into a frenzy. They moved too quickly to be seen as individuals. The scene at the center of the hall was little more than a blur of bodies and weapons, blood and tearing flesh. Knox's magic screamed at him; the others around him shifted restlessly. They stood poised, their knees bent and hands raised, but none of them could figure out what to do or indeed where to direct their magic. They were useless.

"Father," Knox shouted, straining as best he could to make his voice heard above the din. Uilleam, armed with neither magic or claws, ran into the fray with a scream that chilled Knox's very soul. For long moments, everything was chaos. The Mac Tire and the soldiers clashed with claw and sword while on the edges of the room, men and women screamed and scrambled to get out of the way. While Knox and his fellows were too afraid of injuring their own to start firing off magic spells indiscriminately, the Council's Magi had no such qualms. They fired off hex after hex, taking down Mac Tire and their own men without distinction.

"This is madness," Knox said to himself. "Absolute madness." They had the upper hand for the moment, but they were outnumbered and would be overwhelmed in mere minutes. Knox had led Cailean right to his death, fulfilling the exact purpose the Council had set out for him.

"Cailean," Knox said softly, then louder: "Cailean!"

The scope of the battle changed without warning. All of a sudden, the uneven numbers overwhelmed the Mac Tire, and they began to fall. The pale man who had complained of the heat went down first, taking a bolt of magic straight to the chest and crumpling in a heap at Yaara's feet. She let out a roar and bent to help him, providing a perfect target for the Magus's next hex.

Yaara. Tides, Yaara. A black singe mark marred her golden flesh.

"We've got to get out," Knox said. He grabbed the man nearest him and screamed into his ear. "We've got to move! They'll be slaughtered!"

"How?" the man shouted back. "How do we—"

Suddenly, the great doors behind them exploded inward with a racket so deafening the Magus nearest Knox covered his ears and dropped to the ground, shaking all over. Knox spun around, hands out, ready to blast through anyone in the path of safety.

Rhys stood in the wrecked doorway with her hands on her hips. Behind her were men and women, a countless number of them standing elbow to elbow, their faces set in grim determination.

"Rhys," Knox breathed as his heart stumbled and lurched into a frantic rhythm. Of course Rhys had defied her brother. Of course she had. Knox offered up a prayer of thanks. Shouts rippled through the great hall. Rhys stepped forward, and the entire battle seemed to pause as Cailean met her gaze over the confused commotion between them.

"Hello, brother. You need some help?"

FOURTEEN

THE BATTLE spilled out of the great hall and down the steps to the courtyard below. Everywhere Knox looked, men and women were locked in struggle; he couldn't have counted their number if they were standing still, and they certainly weren't. The Magi surrounding him began to move away, joining in the fight where they could. Knox barely paid them any mind. He couldn't look away from the place where Cailean was fending off three men with swords and a Magus who was shouting nonsense. Why did no one help him? Were they so overwhelmed that no one could see Cailean was near to falling?

Knox's promise to Cailean meant nothing, not if he was going to lose Cailean in the process. Heart in his throat, he ran forward. He dodged spells and weapons as he ran. Katrina had joined the battle. She called out to him as he sprinted past; he could not spare her a single moment. His feet were quick, but not quick enough. He had almost reached Cailean, was very nearly there, when all of a sudden Cailean threw back his head and let out a mighty scream. His entire body bowed, his back arching, the tendons in his neck straining. Knox froze and watched in mute terror as the magic spell that had hit Cailean's back tore through his chest.

Knox's magic cried out within him. He stumbled forward, tripping over his own feet. He reached Cailean as he went down, breaking his fall. His hands slipped in the blood that was soaking through Cailean's shirt, but Knox held fast, going down on his knees and pulling Cailean to his chest.

Around them, the battle waged on. It did not lessen in intensity or sound as Knox's world crumbled around him.

"Cailean," he said desperately, wrapping his hands around Cailean's chest and covering the gaping wound as best he could. "Cailean. Look at me. Cailean!"

Cailean blinked at him slowly. "Knox?"

"Cailean, you idiot. What have you done? Oh tides, what have you done?"

"Knox."

"Cailean. Oh no, Cailean." Knox raked his gaze over Cailean's body. He was cut in so many places, and the wound in his chest—he couldn't even begin to know where to start. The spell that had torn open Cailean's chest was still pulsing through him like a dark, ugly thing. Knox wanted to wrap his fist around it and yank it free of Cailean's body. He wanted to cover Cailean's body with his own and press every bit of power and magic and love he had into him. But he was paralyzed as he watched the man he loved bleeding to death in his arms. How could this have happened? How could he have stood on the outskirts of the fight so long that this had happened? And not just today's battle. He'd known for years that the Council's rule was unjust and unkind, and he'd done nothing.

He'd done nothing.

"I told you—"

"Do I look like I bleeding care what you've got to say right now? Do I? God, Cailean. You're—" He choked on the words and shook his head. This couldn't happen. He couldn't let this happen.

"Listen to me," Cailean said. He coughed then, and blood flew from his lips. He grimaced and shook in Knox's arms. "You've got to—got to get out. Get to Rhys. Get her out. Go... you've got to go."

A body landed on the ground near Knox's knees. No, not a body. Only part of one. Men were dying while Knox sat by and did nothing.

"No," Knox said. Then louder: "No." He bent his head low and kissed Cailean's forehead, pressing his mouth to the blood and sweat that marred his pale face. He gently lowered Cailean to the ground and pushed himself to his feet.

He lifted his hands and felt the magic that coursed through him. It called out to him like a song, resonated within him. He closed his eyes and hung his head, letting the force of gravity pull at him until he thought his bones would simply sink into the ground below him. Then he looked up, raised his hands, and called upon the magic within the earth. He dug his hands into the threads of it and wound them around his fingers. They were golden and warm. They were sunshine and warm spring days. Knox pulled and pulled, hunching forward with the force of it. He'd only meant to take enough magic to heal Cailean, did not wish to take all the magic from the earth, but it came anyway, returning to him like an apple falling to the grass.

The ground began to groan beneath him. The first quakes were deep and low, the wind a strong rushing where moments ago there had been only screams and bloodshed. This would not stand. Knox wouldn't allow it.

The fighting came to a confused halt as the air began to whip through the courtyard, throwing everything into an enormous tangle of blurred faces and colors. Knox had the half-formed thought that he should close his eyes against the dirt that tore at the vulnerable skin of his face, but he dismissed the idea before it could take root. Instead he watched in bleary wonder as the ground under their feet began to shift. It fractured with an almighty groan in a line that ran directly to the steps of the great castle. Rocks crumbled and fell into the ravine as men and women screamed and threw their bodies away from the separating ground.

Another crack appeared, then another. From a great distance, someone was shouting Knox's name. He blinked the grit from his eyes and saw Rhys standing just in front of him, her hands cupped around her mouth.

"Knox! Stop! You have to stop!"

"Cailean...."

"Knox."

Like something out of a dream, Knox turned and found Cailean had clambered to his feet. His shirt was still drenched in blood, but his face was no longer cast in the pale white of death. "Knox, you have to stop. Let it go."

"It's—"

"Let it go, Knox."

Clumsily, Knox nodded. He began to flex his fingers, trying to untangle the magic from them. He wanted them free. He wanted to be able to run his hands over Cailean's chest and make sure, make quite sure, that the magic *had* healed him, that he was whole and all right and decidedly not dead. But the magic held fast, and it began to rain, great sheets of it that came out of nowhere and drenched them to the bone within seconds. Around them, people were screaming and running, too afraid to stay still but unsure where to go to escape the chaos.

"Knox!"

Knox blinked the water out of his eyes and looked down to see Cailean's blood-soaked fingers close around his own, even as the rain washed them clean.

"It's enough, Knox. Stop it now."

And just like that, the magic released him. Almost as though it was obeying Cailean, the magic quieted until it was nothing more than a gentle swell in Knox's belly.

Knox squeezed Cailean's hands and blacked out.

WHEN KNOX awoke, his body ached in places he'd never even realized existed. He groaned and rolled over, only to topple off the narrow bed he'd been resting on. "Tides," he muttered, sitting up and rubbing a rueful hand over his head. He looked around. The room he was in was a small chamber outfitted with the bed upon which he had slept, a chair, and a washbasin. The walls were a dark wood.

Uilleam was asleep in the chair, his neck cocked at what had to be an uncomfortable angle. His mouth hung open. He snored gently against his chest. Knox's heart swelled at the sight of him.

"Father."

Knox clattering out of bed hadn't done it, but the sound of his son's voice snatched Uilleam from sleep, and he jerked awake. "Knox," he said hoarsely. "Knox, you're awake. And... on the floor."

"I fell out of the bed."

Uilleam shook his head. "Of course you did," he said, pushing himself to his feet and reaching out to offer Knox a hand. He pulled him up and wrapped him in a hug. "You scared the shit out of me, kid."

"I scared the shit out of me too."

"Are you all right?" Uilleam ran his hands all over Knox, feeling him for any unseen injuries. "Are you hurt?"

"I'm fine," Knox said, though a large part of him wanted to curl up into a tiny ball and let his father protect him from the world for a while. Everything that had happened over the last few weeks was catching up with him, and Knox felt he could happily crawl back into the bed and sleep for a week or two. But the larger part of him needed to see Cailean, to touch him and know that he was all right.

Uilleam must have read it on his face, because he smiled and patted Knox on the chest. "Cailean and Rhys are meeting with the Council."

"They're *what*?" Knox grabbed for his boots, which were tucked beside the bed, but Uilleam caught him with a hand to the crook of his arm.

"He's fine, Knox. You wouldn't believe how eager the Council was to come to terms for peace after you nearly drowned the entire city. Cailean is drawing up maps and moving the Council, and those loyal to them, down to the grasslands. There isn't enough room in the dungeons for them, and Cailean seems to think that if they can make a living in the grasslands, they can have the land."

"Oh," Knox said. "He doesn't think they'll rise against the kingdom again?"

"No, they will," Uilleam said. "But this is as close to peace as we're likely to get. Hopefully there will be time enough for... well." Uilleam shook his head. "Tides, I remember when you having a chat with Egan was the worst of our troubles."

"Egan! Is she—they'll have sold her, haven't they?"

Uilleam shook his head. "She's as right as tides. Cathal's been keeping her in his stables. He said he'll keep her for you until you find a place for her to stay."

"Cathal?" Knox asked in disbelief. "What on earth has Cathal to do with anything? How long have I been asleep?"

Uilleam laughed. "I have so much to tell you. Cathal has been working with the Resistance for years," Uilleam said. "He's been spying on them and passing word to the Resistance and to the Mac Tire."

Knox shook his head. Surely his brain had rattled loose. "He never has."

"He got those maps to you, didn't he? We've been trying to discover a weak point in the ráth for years. If we hadn't gotten a hold of those…." He trailed off and shrugged. "His mother was a Magus. The Council used her at the beginning. She spread word through Ailis that the Mac Tire—" He sneered. "The beasts were planning to wage war on the humans. She used her magic on people so that they would believe her and spread her lies. On her deathbed, she told Cathal the truth. He's been with us ever since."

Knox sat down on the bed, unable to believe his ears. He would have sooner believed up was down and left was right. Exhaustion began to darken the edges of his vision, and he sunk down into the pillows, allowing a half grin to tug at his mouth when Uilleam moved to tuck the blankets in around him.

"What of the others?"

Grief clouded Uilleam's face.

"Cailean and Rhys are both fine. I saw Clive."

Uilleam nodded. "And a few others. Fewer than we'd thought."

With eyes pressed shut, Knox asked the question whose answer he dreaded. "Yaara?"

"She's alive, but only just. She took a dark hex to her heart. She's… well. There are physicians with her. "

Knox took in a deep breath. He couldn't have said how he knew it, but he could help her. He was sure. "I'd like to see her. I think I can help."

Uilleam looked relieved. "I was hoping you'd say that. We've been praying for you to awaken. I know you've done so much already, but if you can help—"

"I can. And I want to. Just—" With some untapped store of strength, he pushed himself upright. "Help me out of bed?"

The door opened, and Cailean walked in. Knox nearly toppled out of the bed again. He had changed his shirt but hadn't bathed; there was dried blood crusted on his neck and in the crooks of his fingers, but Knox didn't care. He didn't think he'd ever seen anything better in his entire life.

"Cailean," Knox breathed. "You're all right."

"Thanks to you," Cailean said. He walked over and sat beside Knox, reaching up and brushing Knox's hair off his forehead. "Though you nearly wrecked my kingdom in the process."

"*Your* kingdom?"

"The Elders are drawing up the treaty now. All of our lands are returning to us. Some of the Council members are in the prisons, the others are gathering what they can carry. Has your father told you…?"

"The meadowlands," Knox supplied. "Do you feel that's wise?"

"It feels fair. I won't become the beast they wish I was. There will be trials, but she is my kingdom." He smiled and ducked his head. "Well. Ours. You couldn't have done what you did if the land didn't respond to your magic."

Knox leaned forward and folded himself against Cailean's body. He leaned into his broad chest and rested there, listening to the reassuring beat of life beneath his cheek. "I don't care about any of that."

Cailean huffed a soft laugh. "Liar."

The door clicked shut behind Uilleam. Left alone, Knox wanted nothing more than to strip Cailean of all of his clothes and wash his skin, to find any place in need and press his magic there until Cailean couldn't even remember what pain felt like. But there were other things that needed his attention more.

"I want to see to Yaara," Knox murmured. "Father says she is unwell."

"She's stabilized. She asked after you."

"Where is she?"

"In the old physician's rooms. I'll take you there." He pressed a kiss to Knox's knuckles. "I want to show you something. It's on the way."

CAILEAN LED him from the room and down a long stone corridor lit with brightly burning torches. The corridor opened up to a larger hallway, and then another. They walked down the long hallway with their hands clasped tight together. Knox didn't care if he looked foolish, dressed in his sleeping clothes and barefoot. He'd be damned if he ever let Cailean out of his sight again.

They came to the end of the corridor. Cailean unlatched the heavy door he found there and pushed it open. He stepped back and motioned for Knox to step outside.

"What's this?"

"This used to be the main courtyard," Cailean said. "Before." He gave Knox a long, searching look, then turned and pointed to the center of the courtyard where a large stone, at least ten feet in height, arched toward the blue sky. It was surrounded by a ring of smaller stones, each of which could have seated two men. It was a place groaning under the weight of magic. It drenched every inch of the courtyard and poured out of the stones, nearly knocking Knox over with its intensity. It hummed with the same sort of powerful red energy that seeped out of Cailean's skin. "Lia Fáil," Knox breathed. "It is, isn't it?"

"I thought they'd have destroyed it. But I don't think they could. You saw they used the south entrance to the castle instead of this one. I think it was because they couldn't stand this one."

"Have you...." Knox glanced from the stone back to Cailean. "Have you touched it?"

Cailean shook his head. "Not yet. I was waiting on you."

"You don't want to wait for Rhys?"

"Not if… Knox, what if nothing happens? What if it doesn't cry out for me?" It was as uncertain as Knox had ever seen Cailean, and something in him thrilled to be allowed to see him laid so bare.

"It will," Knox said, grabbing Cailean's hands and squeezing them as tightly as he could. "It will. Of course it will. It has to."

With a shuddering breath, Cailean nodded. He pressed one more kiss to their clasped hands, then straightened his shoulders and moved toward the stone. Knox stepped back and waited, breath high in his chest. His heart tripped over itself. Cailean knelt down by the stone and raised his hands held in front of him. He bowed his head and waited there. His chest heaved. It was as intimate a thing as Knox had ever witnessed. It surely hadn't ever been meant for human eyes. Still, Cailean wanted him here. That was all that mattered.

"Come on," Knox murmured. "Come on, come on. Cry out for him, please. You have to."

Cailean reached out his battle-scarred hands, smeared with tears and blood, worn from battle and danger and life, and rested them on the stone.

Rhys had been wrong. The stone didn't cry out.

When the rightful king of Ailis placed his hands upon it, Lia Fáil roared.

JENNI MICHAELS has loved to make up stories since she was a little girl, hiding under the blankets with her sister armed with nothing more than a flashlight and her imagination. Now that she's a grown-up, she likes to write them down.

Jenni lives on the outskirts of Atlanta, Georgia, with her husband, their son, and a retired racing greyhound whose proudest achievement is mastering the command "Be my little spoon." She loves reading, writing, hiking, traveling, quilting, and learning. She loves to make new friends, especially the kind who want to talk about books. You can find her on Twitter and on Tumblr. Come and say hi! Bring cookies!

Twitter: @EditorJenn
Tumblr: lovejennimichaels.com

Matthew Bryson spends his days working quietly and wishing for a chance to explore another side of himself. When he gathers the nerve to post on a BDSM message board, Matthew meets Evan Haynes, a Dom recently removed from the scene after a messy break-up with his boyfriend/sub.

Evan and Matthew enter into a tentative D/s relationship, but only Matthew receives gratification. Still shaken from his experience, Evan refuses sexual reciprocation from Matthew, afraid he'll grow too close. While Evan is the perfect Dom to satisfy Matthew's needs, he finds it harder than he anticipated to keep Matthew at a distance, and it eventually becomes more than he can bear.

http://www.dreamspinnerpress.com

BLOODY ARIA

Lorraine Ulrich

http://www.dreamspinnerpress.com

FAMILY OF LIES
SEBASTIAN

SAM ARGENT

http://www.dreamspinnerpress.com

The Guardian's Destiny

Fil Preis

http://www.dreamspinnerpress.com

IMMORTAL

AMY LANE

http://www.dreamspinnerpress.com

Cassie Sweet

Kiss of Death

ALCHEMISTS AND ELEMENTALS BOOK THREE

http://www.dreamspinnerpress.com

SHIRA ANTHONY

MERMEN OF EA
RUNNING
with the WIND

http://www.dreamspinnerpress.com

ANNE MOK

Tower

OF THE ICE LORD

http://www.dreamspinnerpress.com